The Greatcoat

By the same author

HELEN DUNMORE

The Greatcoat

Atlantic Monthly Press
New York

First published in Great Britain in 2012 by Hammer Books
an imprint of Random House Group Limited

Printed in the United States of America

ISBN 978-0-8021-2060-1

Atlantic Monthly Press
an imprint of Grove/Atlantic, Inc.
841 Broadway
New York, NY 10003

Distributed by Publishers Group West

www.groveatlantic.com

12 13 14 15   10 9 8 7 6 5 4 3 2 1

To Jane

The Greatcoat

Prologue

It was six-thirty; two and a half hours since briefing. The men stood around outside the locker room, waiting for crew buses to take them to the aircraft at their dispersals. All day it had been raining, off and on. Cold, wintry East Riding rain. At three the cloud had hung so low that the treetops were hidden. It looked as if ops would be scrubbed again, but then a light wind chased the murk away. They were on. They were going to the big city.

In the locker room earlier, Alec had given Jimmy a ten-bob note. Jimmy had stared at it blankly.

'What's this, Skip?'

'You won your bet, remember?'

Jimmy folded the note and stowed it carefully with his valuables, in his locker. He'd given his winnings to Alec for safe keeping, so he wouldn't drink them. Now the ten-bob note was locked away with the letter to Phyll he'd written years ago, it seemed; but it was really only months ago, before the crew's first op. It wasn't the kind of letter he'd want her to keep, if it came to that. He hadn't known what to put. He ought to write another, a proper letter she and the kid could be proud of, but he hadn't got round to it.

'Bloody jammy bastard,' said Douggie. 'I'd have made you go two hundred yards.'

'Bloody good navigation if you ask me,' said Jimmy. He was only twenty-two but he had a wife and baby, and ten bob was ten bob. He'd cycled a hundred yards in a straight line with a WAAF on the handlebars, another on the crossbar and a third pillion, and had won his bet. Balance had been the problem but they'd been grounded for two days by fog, and intensive training had paid off.

'Bang on,' said Alec.

Jimmy and Les lit cigarettes, heads together. Laney, next to Alec, began to growl under his breath to the tune of 'Deutschland, Deutschland über Alles':

We don't want to go to Chopland
We don't want to go at all
We don't want to go to Chopland
Where our chances are f***-all . . .

No one reacted. It was what Laney did every time, before they got on the crew bus. Now buses pulled up and crew names were shouted into the raw dark. Alec's stomach burned as it always did. He knew it would stop as soon as he was back inside K-Katie. His mind was fogged with thoughts of Elizabeth but he knew that they too would dissolve. He would be clear as he always was, checking instruments, inter-com, controls.

'Got your gloves, Skip?'

'Got my gloves,' Alec confirmed.

His silk gloves were lucky. Each time he climbed into Katie he touched her with them. Each of the crew had his own luck, but they all believed in the Skipper's gloves. He wore them under two other pairs: chamois leather and wool. He never wore his gauntlets. They were clumsy, and in them he couldn't get a feel for the controls. He didn't tell his crew about the other good-luck charm, the private one.

The men swayed in the dim blue light as the bus bounced along the perimeter track. He watched the back of the Waaf who was driving. She had red hair and a big freckly smile for them when they had clambered on, heavy in their flying kit. No one spoke. They were wound up now and they needed to be doing. He checked his crew over in his mind. Jimmy OK, Douggie OK, Les you never had to ask, Syd was

AI again after missing two ops due to a throat infection, Laney OK – but for the whole two days Rod hadn't been able to stop binding on about the fog. Alec had said nothing, but he'd heard the edge in Rod's voice and seen the quick, cautious way the others glanced at him. The fog had been bad for everyone. They were too near the end of their tour now, and they didn't want to be messed around. Twenty-seventh op tonight; after tonight, only three to go. You just wanted it over but you knew you couldn't think like that. Trying to get things over with was what led to mistakes. Ops being posted and then scrubbed got on everyone's nerves. You started thinking: If we'd gone ahead last night then we'd be on twenty-eight now, only two more to go after tonight. *Tour expired.* Even to think about it was dangerous. It was like looking directly at the Aldis lamp as you taxied down the runway, instead of letting it register at the side of your field of vision. That was the way to lose the sharpness you'd built up: the power to see into the dark that swelled all the way from here to Berlin. He wasn't going to make that mistake.

You stupid bastard, he told himself, you're already making it.

Chapter One

1952

Isabel sat back on her heels and watched flames spring up in the grate. They were pale and there was no heat in them. She was cold, she was tired, her back ached and her eyes stung – from the smoke, of course. But at least the fire was lit. As long as she looked only at the blue and yellow flames, she could begin to feel at home. The room was so dark, even with the light on. It was crammed with furniture and it smelled of Brussels sprouts.

Philip opened the door. His arms were piled with medical textbooks, right up to his chin. His eyes searched Isabel's face as she turned to him.

'Are you warming up a bit?'

'I'm fine.'

'You're too thin, that's what it is.'

'I'm not one of your patients, Philip.'

Awkwardly, as he watched, she stood up.

'I went to the butcher and got a meat pie, just as they were closing,' said Philip proudly. 'It was off the ration.'

'You didn't!' He had braved the queue of head-scarved women, all looking sideways at him and maybe clicking their tongues at his presence. *Eh, dear, what's his wife thinking of?* He hadn't cared about his dignity, or the fact that although they might not yet know he was the new doctor, come to work in Dr Ingoldby's practice, they would recognise him soon enough. Isabel reached out and touched Philip's hand. 'That was very clever of you,' she said.

His lean face softened. 'You only need to put it in the oven,' he said.

'I brought the potatoes with us,' said Isabel, 'and those carrots. They're a bit old, but I cut out the worst bits.'

They had been children of wartime and all they asked of food was that it should fill them. Isabel was a poor cook. Fortunately Philip's mother was no better, and after years of national service and medical school, he was hardened. He never complained, and he was as proud as Isabel when she brought her watery stews and dense cakes to the table.

They had been married for two months. This was

their first home together, after an eight-week eternity of living with Philip's parents in their narrow house where bed springs cracked like whips and the flush of the lavatory was the bellow of a caged water-dragon. His parents wanted Isabel to call them Mother and Father, as if she and Philip were still children, and siblings. But they were grown-ups. Philip had his first job. Isabel would set up home.

'I'll be working all the hours God sends,' Philip had warned her.

Footsteps crossed the floor above their heads. Slow, heavy, deliberate. All the way to the window they went, and all the way back. The landlady. Philip knew her, because he had handled the negotiations for the flat. The rent was too high, but with the housing shortage it was what you had to expect. Isabel had only glimpsed Mrs Atkinson's ponderous back-view, clad in a grey working pinafore, disappearing upstairs. That was her idea of welcome, evidently. Their flat was on the ground floor, with a sitting room that looked over the road, a bedroom at the back, and off the bedroom a pokey kitchen with a wooden-lidded bath taking up most of the space. There was a cloakroom in the hall: you had to go out of the flat each time you wanted what the landlady called 'the facilities'.

'The facilities are shared,' she had told Philip grimly. 'No personal effects are to be left there.'

'I don't see why. There aren't any other tenants,' Philip told Isabel.

'She doesn't want me to hang up my knickers in there.'

The hall was dankly cold. How am I going to live here? Isabel asked herself, and her thoughts plummeted, as they sometimes did, until everything was dark. She fumbled with the lights, fumbled with the cistern chain and had to yank it down twice before it would flush. She thought of herself going in and out at bedtime, with a spongebag containing her toothbrush and a flannel. The landlady was still walking overhead, back and forth. Isabel shivered.

I can't live here, she almost said to Philip as she came back into the flat. But he was building up the fire and he glanced up at her with such a smile, a naked smile full of hope and doubt, that she said, 'I'm going to make new covers for the chairs. I can buy material in the market. That will cheer the place up.'

Their bed was vast. They lay still between hummocks of ticking-covered mattress. The iron springs settled beneath them, and there was a faint smell – not unpleasant; just old, Isabel thought. Old polish, old furniture, old dust, and all those many, many nights that other people had slept on this bed. Who were they? Did they lie awake, entwined, whispering, laughing, or did they sleep coldly, each one irritated by the sounds the other made?

If she were at home she would have dragged the mattress out onto the lawn, slung it over chairs and then beaten it until the dust flew and the sweetness of the air got into it. She could remember her mother doing that. But home had ended when Isabel was eight and she went to live with her aunt and uncle because her parents were going out to Singapore. Her father worked for the McPhail Rubber Company. As soon as they were settled, her mother said, Isabel would be coming out to join them.

Isabel could still see her mother beating the mattress furiously, her soft face set stern. But did that ever really happen? How could she have hauled such a heavy thing all the way downstairs? Someone must have helped, but Isabel's memory had so many holes in it. She had to trust it, though, because she had nothing else.

Philip was asleep. Jealously, Isabel cleared her throat and wriggled until her legs touched his. She was icy. If the flat was like this in September, what would it be like in January? She crept closer to him, but he muttered busily, as if he were writing a prescription for one of his patients, and did not wake.

In the morning Philip left for the surgery at eight, after riddling and stoking the kitchen stove. Isabel watched him. She had to learn how to do everything. Unlike Philip, she hadn't grown up laying fires, fetching in coal and wood, earning money after school and on Saturdays. She was soft: 'nesh' he said, when he was teasing her. By ten o'clock she had made the bed, washed up and laid their clothes in the drawers of the ugly old chest. Upstairs, the landlady coughed. Too close, thought Isabel. They had divided the house into flats but they couldn't quite separate the lives within it.

Outside the windows an early mist was thinning. There would be sun. She would go shopping. Her aunt had bought her a book called *Early Days: An Introduction to Housekeeping for the Young Wife*. It advised that 'the young wife must make a friend of her butcher, fishmonger and greengrocer'.

Certainly, thought Isabel, she had no other friends in the town. She might as well start with a rubicund butcher whose hands dripped with the tang of blood. She picked up her handbag and snapped its clasp with a fat, important click. She was a little girl

THE GREATCOAT

pretending to be her mother. She would sally forth with her mother's smile, to coax an extra slice of bacon or assess a piece of cod. If the fish were whole, you could tell how fresh it was from the brightness of its eyes, or so it said in the book. Isabel studied its pages as once she'd studied Milton and Molière. There were no more essays to write or exams to pass. How she missed those clear, sure channels towards the light. She'd done so well in her Higher School Cert that Miss Bellamy had wanted her to try for a university place.

You could have taught, she told herself. You could have taken the Civil Service exams. You chose to marry Philip.

The minster leaned over the end of the street like a black ship. It was beautiful, of course. The shops were in the other direction, in the warren of narrow streets where – somewhere – there was also the marketplace.

At the butcher's, there was no beef. Mutton or pork was on offer. There was tripe, and kidneys which smelled faintly of urine. The long queue of solid women looked Isabel up and down. Isabel gave over the ration books, and the butcher stamped them. Seven years after the end of the war, and you still had to bite back your protest when the butcher weighed down the scales with fat. Philip's mother had stressed that it was vital to keep in with the butcher.

She would go home, put the fatty parcel into the meat safe and then she would change into her walking shoes and go out of the town, as far as she could, where there were no shops or houses or watchful, secretive faces. She would walk until even the minster was out of sight.

The town ended suddenly, and Isabel was out on the dusty road, between hedges where the leaves were already turning. The land was flat and it spread for miles under hazy autumn sunlight. Isabel walked fast, pushing the miles away from her. The road was wide, for a country lane. Two lorries could pass easily, but the verges were growing over the tarmac, narrowing it, as if its width wasn't needed any more.

She had been walking for an hour and a half. The town was hidden by a faint swell in the landscape behind her. She must have come four miles, perhaps five. She could hear nothing but birds, tractors, and the wind soughing in the hedges. Somewhere in this vast landscape Philip was doing his rounds after morning surgery. No one on earth knew where she was.

As she rounded the next corner the road widened again. Ahead of her stretched a perimeter fence that went on as far as she could see. But it was broken down in places, and the wide gates swung open. She knew at once what it was. Isabel came from the flatlands of Suffolk, and during her wartime childhood she had woken night after night to the thunder of Lancasters overhead, as they took off from the airfield. The noise seemed to go on for hours, before the last of the aircraft throbbed beyond her hearing. Once, Isabel had been up with earache when the thunder began. Her aunt had grown still, listening: 'There they go, Isabel.' Aunt Jean had drawn back the blackout and let Isabel see the lights of the aircraft. 'There won't be any lights,' she said, 'once they're over enemy territory.' The black bombers would be hidden against the black sky. Bombers from all over the east of England would assemble somewhere over the coast, and then the bombing stream would head eastwards, over Holland and on into Germany, towards the Ruhr or the deep heartland of Berlin. Long hours later, they would return; or most of them would. Her aunt would listen for them in the hours before dawn.

Isabel and her cousin Charlie had been taken out to see the airfield when it was still under construction. There was a guardhouse, and Isabel had asked her aunt, 'What would happen if I ran past the guardhouse? Would they say, "Halt, who goes there?"'

Charlie had laughed at her: 'They'd shoot you, Is.'

She hadn't known there was a bomber station so close to Kirby Minster. But of course, that would be why they had widened the road. There must have been lorries pounding over it day and night, servicing the thousands of people who lived out here in their temporary city. Air crew, ground crew, Waafs, everyone from wing commander to cleaners. Already Isabel was walking forward, past the guardhouse. Some of the fence was down. The silence of the deserted airfield folded round her.

Everything was still, but for the wind sifting across concrete. Thistles, dock and willowherb sprouted from cracks. Bramble snaked out of the long grass, and coiled up the fence. Isabel heard her aunt's voice in her head. They were standing close together, the three of them, watching the mud churn as the flat farmland became an airfield.

'That's going to be the control tower. They direct the aircraft from there.'

'Where will the aircraft go?' It was Charlie's voice now.

'They'll be dispersed all around the perimeter,' said her aunt authoritatively. 'They have to do that, in case of German attack. If the aircraft were in one place, they could be destroyed by a single enemy raid. The bomb store is camouflaged, too.'

'What are all those buildings?'

'Admin. Barracks. They have everything they need here.'

Isabel tested the words in her mouth. *Admin.* It sounded mysterious, powerful. 'Do they have houses to sleep in?' she asked babyishly. Charlie grinned and lightly kicked her leg.

Aunt Jean frowned. 'They sleep in Nissen huts,' she said briefly.

Aunt Jean knew everything, because she was on the parish council. She wrestled every bit of knowledge to herself, and gave it out sparingly, to those who deserved it.

Soon the village was full of airmen, as if her aunt's predictions had made them spring into being. There was only one pub, and everybody went there, shouting and singing and spilling out into the summer darkness with beer mugs in their hands. Isabel and Charlie would hang about the green on their bikes, doing endless circuits, watching, listening. Some people in the village grumbled about the invasion, but not Aunt Jean. Strict as she usually was, she had endless tolerance for these young men, and would take to task those who complained about heavy drinking, shadowy couples enlaced by the walls of the village hall, or a young flight lieutenant tearing through the village on his motorbike. On Sundays Aunt Jean invited air crew to tea, to give them a taste of home, she said. Isabel couldn't help knowing that there was nothing very homely about Aunt Jean, or the stiff way in which she set out the best tea things on little tables in the sitting room, instead of comfortably around the kitchen table. Isabel and Charlie were always warned to say that they didn't want any cake. 'It's the least we can do for them,' Aunt Jean said.

On still nights they could hear the aircraft starting up, taxiing, waiting for take-off. Isabel thought of the flight sergeant who had caught her watching hungrily as he took another piece of apple sponge. He had laughed and said, 'On second thoughts . . .' and put it onto her plate. Aunt Jean hadn't been pleased, but Isabel ate it up quickly, before she could be stopped, and all the men laughed.

Isabel was twelve now, Charlie thirteen. They were old enough to understand what was happening, Aunt Jean said, and she let them listen to the radio reports of the bombing raids. They knew what it meant when Alvar Lidell intoned that 'one of our aircraft failed to return'. When the men were on operations, the pub was almost empty.

We used to talk about 'the airfield', as if it were the only one in the country, thought Isabel. But there were dozens, all over Suffolk and Lincolnshire, Leicestershire and East Yorkshire. She looked around her, at the silent, sleeping landscape at peace in the autumn sunlight. There's probably a village near here, too, she thought, with a pub that used to be packed with men in uniform. Now there are only farm-workers again.

Isabel shaded her eyes and scanned the wreck of the airfield. She could pick out the control tower, hangars, admin buildings, roads, Nissen huts. The main runway disappeared into the distance. They hadn't demolished the buildings; they hadn't bothered. They had just left everything to the weather.

A cloud of birds was pecking at something on the ground. They lifted for a second and she saw that it was a dead rabbit, and then they went back to it again, businesslike, working methodically at the soft parts.

Isabel glanced quickly behind her. Of course there was nothing there. It was the atmosphere of the place, that was all.

You're being absurd, she said to herself. She was in the habit of giving herself a good talking-to from time to time. Charlie used to call her a scaredy-cat when she wouldn't follow him on his wilder expeditions. 'You're just a little scaredy-cat,' she said aloud.

The more she looked, the more the immediate impression of a place fit for use faded. Doors were hanging off. There was broken glass that caught the light. Maybe boys from the village came up here and smashed things, now that they could. Or courting couples—

No. No one would come here for love. It wasn't

that sort of place. It would run down a little more and then it would be returned to farmland, like other 'hostilities-only' bomber stations. They would plough up the runways, the dispersal aprons and the perimeter tracks. The shadow of them would be all that remained, like the shadow of an Iron Age fort in photographs taken from the air.

No one in the world knows where I am, thought Isabel again, and this time she shivered a little, because the wind had turned cold now that the autumn afternoon was slipping away. Briskly, as if someone were watching her, she turned and walked away at a steady pace, not looking back. She passed through the gates and was back in the lane. When she reached a curve and the airfield was hidden behind her she walked faster, with the breath of fear on her back, until she was only just not running.

Once the minster came into view, she slowed. She began to regret her own cowardice. You could have gone further, she told herself. You could have gone into the mess huts. You could even have climbed up to the top of the control tower. There was no one to stop you.

Chapter Two

Philip was going to get a car; it was essential with such a big country practice. 'There's the chance of a Ford Prefect,' he told Isabel, with a quirking smile that hid his pride.

'But how can we afford it?' asked Isabel.

'It's ancient. It belonged to one of Dr Ingoldby's patients.'

'Is he going to let you have it cheaply?'

'The old chap's dead, and his wife doesn't drive. I went out to see the car yesterday. It's in wonderful condition, Is! I shouldn't think they've had it out of the garage for years. It'll need new tyres and a complete overhaul, but then it'll go like a bird.'

Isabel did not drive. Perhaps she would learn, but even then, Philip would need the car every day. Once morning surgery in town was over, he would drive miles and miles between scattered villages and isolated farms. It was bare, lonely, rich country. Dr Ingoldby said that Philip had the right stuff in him. He would bat through evening surgery, and then go out on night calls without a murmur. The long hours seemed to stimulate rather than exhaust him. He could get up fresh from four or five hours' sleep, while Isabel blundered around the stove, barely able to speak. Clean-shaven, already in his shirt and tie, Philip looked as if he belonged in a different world from the muddle of the flat. Sometimes, after these early wakings, Isabel would go back to bed in the afternoon, close her eyes and whirl down and down into a pool of darkness from which she woke unrefreshed.

If you're lonely, it's your own fault, said Isabel to herself.

Dr Ingoldby's wife thought Isabel was a nice little thing and asked her to tea in the big, grey house with its shining floors and walled fruit garden. But Janet Ingoldby was fifty. Years of life with Dr Ingoldby had made her guarded, and she said nothing in many words. She talked about her house and her children as if they were a very difficult knitting pattern which Isabel might one day be qualified to follow.

'Are you fond of sewing?' enquired Janet Ingoldby.

'I used to make my own dance dresses.'

Janet Ingoldby frowned at the thought of this. 'You might care to join the sewing circle. But I hear you are bookish. I'm afraid there's not much of that here.'

Philip also wanted Isabel to join things. The thought of her solitude nagged at the back of his mind, until he forgot it in the intensity of his days. There was a young wives' circle. Later there would be the Mothers' Union. Once Isabel had a baby, everything would fall into place.

Every night the landlady trod back and forth, back and forth above Isabel's head. There was no guessing why. She seemed to go nowhere but the shops, and she had no visitors apart from the butcher's and baker's boys. She got up early and went to bed late. She criss-crossed the upstairs rooms like a guard on patrol.

'You are an over-dramatic idiot,' Isabel told herself. She would get a grip, and start living: it was what she had come here to do. She opened *Early Days* and stared at its brisk pages with unseeing eyes. There was a cabbage lurking in the kitchen cupboard, the size of a man's head. There must be a way of cooking it which would not saturate the flat with the dank smell of winter days at school. As if a teacher had called her to attention, Isabel bent over her book. Words jumped at her from the text: haggis, tripe, liver and onions. There was a picture of a cow, standing at grass, and on it were drawn all the cuts of meat it would provide. Isabel turned the pages. She would make a cake. Philip liked cake, and the smell of baking. He would open the door and say, '*This* is like coming home.' *Home* was not a word she would use herself yet, but she liked to hear him say it. One night he'd said to her, 'Have you written to your family yet, Is, to tell them about the flat?' Her face must have shown blank, because he added quickly, 'Of course not, you've been too busy.'

'You are my family, Philip,' she'd said.

Every day it grew colder. Often there was fog, and then the first frost came, writing on the windows and blackening the last few flowers. All the leaves fell from the trees. Philip had to crawl along the lanes with his headlamps full on, nosing his way through the blind whiteness. At night, Isabel piled on all the blankets. Often she went to bed before Philip was back, huddled around her hot water bottle, not daring to stretch out into the icy reaches of the bed.

'If only coal would come off the ration, I might have some chance of getting this place warm,' she said to Philip. 'It's all the draughts. Listen to how those windows rattle.'

'We won't be here for ever,' he assured her. 'I meant to tell you, Dr Ingoldby says he can get us a load of logs from one of his patients—'

'How much?'

'He'll fill the car boot for two shillings.'

But the logs did not materialise. Perhaps they went elsewhere, or else the patient died. One day, as Isabel was filling a scuttle with coal from the bunker allocated to the flat, the landlady came out. Mrs Atkinson's own bunkers were padlocked: one for coke and one for coal. She peered inside Isabel's coal bunker and clicked her tongue.

'That's to last the winter. There'll be no more once it's gone,' she warned grimly.

Nosey old bitch, thought Isabel. She never wanted to look Mrs Atkinson in the face; a quick sideways glance was enough. The landlady was all grey: grey pinafore, greying hair rolled up tightly in a style that had been out of fashion for ten years, seamed face, pursed lips with tiny wrinkles all around them. It was impossible to guess how old she was.

'The kitchen sink keeps blocking,' said Isabel coldly.

'Haven't you got a plunger?'

'I'll have a look,' said Isabel, losing her nerve.

'I should think you'd know if you had one or not.'

'Is it not supplied? This is a furnished flat,' said

Isabel with a flash of fire. My God, she thought, it's come to this. Standing in a backyard, arguing the toss over a sink plunger. She's only our landlady, she has no right to talk to me like this.

'Excuse me,' she said, moving towards the yard entrance. For a moment it seemed as if the landlady wouldn't budge. She was a big woman, a powerful woman; close up, Isabel could see that she wasn't so old. She was staring at Isabel with peculiar concentration, as if there were something the landlady wanted of her, and wasn't sure that she would get. There was a faint, sour smell of sweat. 'Excuse me,' said Isabel again, with more emphasis, as she made to step past Mrs Atkinson, and this time the other woman did stand aside, but not as if Isabel had won the battle of the bunker: no. Her whole face was a jibe, a jeer, so intent and watchful was she, as if every atom of Isabel's being were exposed to her.

'I don't like that woman,' Isabel said to Philip when he came home.

'Who?' he asked absently, putting down his case.

'Our landlady. Mrs Atkinson. If there ever *was* a Mr Atkinson. Perhaps she's got a fancy-man tucked away upstairs. She never lets him out, of course. No one else sees him — he exists for her alone,' and she smiled at her own fantasy, thinking of the landlady's grey face and upright body.

But Philip frowned. 'He's dead. She's a widow. Her husband was—'

'One of Dr Ingoldby's patients, I suppose,' said Isabel. 'I'm surprised any patients still come to him, so many seem to die—'

'You mustn't say that, Is!'

'No one can hear us except Mrs Atkinson. She likes *you*, you know. As soon as you come in, she's flat on the floor listening to us. She probably uses a glass to magnify the sound of our voices.'

'She's not that bad.'

'Isn't she? My God, Phil, what's that?'

It oozed in his hand. A bloody packet, like a wrapped-up heart.

'Steak.'

'From one of the patients?'

Philip nodded.

'But no logs yet?'

'If we drive out to Ellerton at the weekend, they'll fill up the boot.'

'That'll be one in the eye for Mrs Atkinson. Us with a roaring fire and nothing she can do to stop it.'

'We won't be here long, Is. If we can keep on saving like this, we'll have the deposit for our own house by the end of next year.'

'I don't like her, Phil,' said Isabel again, wishing he could believe how serious she was. 'Can't we find somewhere else? There must be other flats.'

'With two big rooms like these? You've got no idea, Isabel. We were lucky to get it.' He thought, but did not say, that it hadn't been Isabel who had tramped from house to house, looking at pokey rooms with lethal cookers and tiny, inadequate grates, breathing in damp and mildew and the faint, unmistakeable smell of bedbugs. Isabel had no idea. He didn't want her to have any idea, ever.

We'll have children, thought Isabel. I'll have a baby and we'll move to a house in one of the villages. A house in the country, with a garden for the pram. I'll put the baby to sleep under the rowan tree. She seemed to see herself looking out of a sunlit kitchen doorway, checking that the baby was fast asleep. But even there, she wasn't alone. Above her head, someone was still walking to and fro.

That night they fell asleep in each other's arms. Hours later, it was cramp in her right hand that woke Isabel. Philip had rolled over and was lying on her arm. Carefully, she freed herself. She had fallen asleep warm, but now she was cold again. The blankets had gathered on Philip's side of the bed, as they always did.

She would have to find something more to put on the bed. She would search the cupboards. She couldn't spend the rest of the night shivering like this. Isabel got up, felt for her slippers on the lino and wrapped Philip's dressing gown tightly around her. She drew back the curtain and stared out at the yard and the tall house backs. There were frost-flowers on the inside of the window, blooming from the corners. A cat skidaddled along a wall, fast as a whippet. It was three in the morning.

Isabel tiptoed into the living room, and put on the light. There was still a little warmth from the fire, but they no longer banked up the grate at night. There wasn't enough coal left. Shortages, restrictions, rules and ration books, coupons and exhortations . . . It had all been going on for as long as Isabel could remember, and there seemed no reason for it ever to stop. People grumbled that if the government had its way, there'd be coal rationing for ever. *You'd never guess who won the war. We're worse off than they are in Germany,* they said.

There was a tall, built-in cupboard in the corner of the room. Isabel had filled most of its shelves with books, because there were no bookcases in the flat. On the top shelf were a pair of pre-war quality curtains that Aunt Jean had given her.

'I could use one of those as a bedcover,' Isabel thought. But there was another box cupboard above, with a separate door, too high for Isabel to reach. Philip had put his old textbooks up there. She remembered him saying that there was some other stuff in the cupboard, but he'd shoved it to the back.

'What kind of stuff?' she'd asked, idly curious.

'I don't know. I didn't look. It felt like old clothes or something. Heavy, anyway.'

That top cupboard was just the kind of place where the landlady might store possessions that she didn't want her tenants to use. It could be clothes, but it might be blankets. Perhaps even a quilt? Isabel was seized by an urge to explore the cupboard. All at once, she was lit up with energy. After all, whatever was there belonged to the flat, and should be for Isabel and Philip to use.

But first, she would have a look at the curtains. She fetched them down and unfolded them. They were thinner than she remembered; when she was a child she had hidden in their folds, imagining herself safe and warm. But they were ordinary lined cotton curtains and would be no use as bedcovers. Isabel folded them up again, disappointed, but also faintly excited. There was good reason for her to search the top cupboard now. She could almost hear herself saying to Philip: I thought Aunt Jean's curtains might do, but they were hopeless. Wasn't it lucky that I thought of looking up at the top?

Isabel fetched one of the dining chairs, kicked off her slippers and clambered onto it. She could reach into the top cupboard, but she couldn't see inside it properly. She felt the hard edges of Philip's books. But as she reached around, her hands met space where she'd expected a wall. The cupboard was bigger than it appeared from the outside, and L-shaped. It went back deep into the wall, but she couldn't reach so far. Philip would have pushed everything right to the back.

Isabel took out three of the thickest textbooks, climbed off her chair and piled the books onto the seat. She tested them with her hand to see if they would slide when she stood on them. They were not very stable, but she'd always had good balance. If only she had the torch, but it was on Philip's bedside table, beside the telephone, in case he had a call in the night. He could get up almost without waking Isabel.

She steadied herself carefully on the pile of books, gripping the edge of the cupboard. Now she could reach inside. Her hand entered space, brushed the sides of the cupboard and came out smeared with cobwebs. She still couldn't reach right around the corner, where Philip would have shoved whatever else was up there, in order to fit in his books. Yes, it was exactly the kind of place where a woman like Mrs Atkinson would hide things . . .

Isabel rose on tiptoe and clung to a shelf as the chair rocked. Any moment she could come crashing down. But if she could get just a little more height she would be able to feel right to the back of it—

Her hand touched cloth. There *was* something there, just as Philip had said. Cunning Mrs Atkinson hadn't been quite cunning enough, thought Isabel in triumph. But whatever it was, it was still too far back and she couldn't quite pull it forward. One more book ought to do it. She swung herself down, hefted a tome on surgical procedure onto her pile and clambered up again.

She was there. Her hand seized a thick fold of cloth and pulled the thing towards her. It came at her in a rush and was in her arms, almost toppling her backwards. How was she to get down with it? She couldn't climb down safely with her arms full . . . but if she bent her knees and jumped sideways, it was really only a few feet down to the floor. She was less likely to hurt herself in a jump than a fall.

The dust flew as Isabel jumped. The jar went through her knees and spine as she landed but she did not topple over. She was on the ground, and the bundle fell open, spreading itself on the floor. She crouched, listening for Philip, in case the noise had woken him. Silence.

It was a coat. An RAF officer's greatcoat, she saw at once, recognising it with a thud of memory. There was the heavy, slatey grey-blue wool, the buttons, the belt with its heavy brass buckle. It had been folded up for a long time, she thought. There was cobweb on the outside but when she unfolded it, the cloth was clean. It was so heavy. The coat felt stiff without a body to shape and warm it. She would shake out the dust and then brush it down.

Isabel went lightly to the door of the flat, unlocked it and was in the hall, carrying the coat. But the front door was locked and bolted. She would make too much noise opening it, she decided. The house was very still but she glanced behind her, fearing that upstairs the landlady might have opened her door noiselessly and be standing there on the landing. This was just the kind of thing she would have been waiting for all those days and nights: evidence of wrongdoing by her tenants.

Isabel returned to the flat, unfastened the big sash window in the living room and pushed it up. A flood of freezing air surrounded her. She lifted the heavy coat, bundled it over the sill and let it out into the night. She flapped and shook it, making the dust fly off into the darkness. It was so heavy. It pulled as if it would tug itself free. She held it tight with one hand and beat it with the other, beating out of it the mustiness of the cupboard which had imprisoned it for so long.

When the greatcoat was back in the room Isabel held it close, up to her face, and for the first time breathed in the smell of it. There was a dry reek of mothballs, and old, woollen cloth. But there was also a faint, acrid tang of burning, and then a smell which flooded Isabel with her childhood. Long grass; sweet hay; the prickle of stalks on the back of her bare legs as she lay and looked up into the vast, polished East Anglian sky. She heard the drowsy chirr of crickets, and the skirl of skylarks. She lay there hidden, like a hare in its form. She was perfectly happy. Far off another noise began: deep, thunderous. She knew that they were testing the engines.

Slowly, Isabel lifted her head and came back to the room. It was impossible that a greatcoat bundled away in a cupboard for years could smell of summer fields.

It must belong to the landlady. She wouldn't want Isabel to have found it, or why hide it so carefully? Perhaps she'd put it away and forgotten about it.

The coat would be so warm. Even now its heavy wool shielded Isabel from the chill of the room. Suddenly, without giving herself time to think, Isabel untied the cord of Philip's dressing gown. Underneath it she was naked. She slipped her arms into the coat and put it on. It settled around her, falling into heavy folds. It was much too big for her, but she'd known that it would be. She was lost in it. Her bare feet stuck out palely. She fingered the buttons and stroked her hand down the texture of the cloth. Warm as the coat was, she shivered, and, as quickly as she had put it on, Isabel stripped it off again. She picked Philip's dressing gown off the floor, pulled it on and tied the cord tightly.

All this while, Philip slept. She went to the door that led through into the bedroom. Light fell on the bed, but he did not stir. She felt her heart tighten, as if he were a child, sleeping there in his innocence, oblivious to the light, to the noise of the coat falling, to Isabel herself. She crept closer to the bedside. His face looked carved in stillness. She could barely hear him breathe. He had flung up one arm behind his head and he lay on his back, occupying the bed as if Isabel had no place in it, or in his dreams. The telephone squatted beside him blackly, like a toad. If it rang, she knew his eyes would snap open and he would begin to speak sensibly, professionally, asking questions, listening intently, almost before he could have begun to think. It was a miracle to her how Philip could come back to himself, shrugging away the place of sleep that too often held Isabel like a hostage, even in the middle of the day.

She stood watching him for a long time, half fearing that her gaze would wake him, half afraid that it would not. At last she spread the coat on her side of the bed, laying claim to it. As if he felt its touch, Philip stirred and rolled away from her and from the greatcoat. He was on his side, still sleeping, with an armful of blanket heaved over his shoulder.

The lino was icy. She shouldn't have left her slippers in the other room. Shuddering, Isabel eased her cold self between the sheets. The greatcoat came down over her, moulding itself to her, pressing her into the mattress.

She woke with light in her eyes like splinters. Philip had pulled the curtains back and was standing by the window, fixing his cufflinks.

'You brute,' grumbled Isabel.

'It's ten to eight. I'm off in a minute. What is that thing on the bed?'

'I found it in the cupboard. I was freezing.'

He came close and peered at it. 'Good lord. Where on earth has that come from?'

Isabel recognised the echo of Dr Ingoldby's voice and phrasing. Philip was going up in the world, she thought to herself, and then quenched the thought for its disloyalty.

'Mrs Atkinson's cupboard. Do you think she'd mind?'

'I shouldn't think so. If she cared about it, she'd have kept it with her, upstairs.'

'So do you think it's all right to put it on the bed? She won't go mad with rage when she next sneaks in here to have a poke around when I'm out?'

'For heaven's sake, Is, it weighs a ton and it must be full of dust.'

'I like it. It's cosy.'

'Besides, what do you mean about Mrs A. poking about?'

'I'm sure she does. Everything looks wrong sometimes, when I come back. As if someone's moved things, and been very careful to put them back in the right places, but not quite careful enough. No, that's not quite right – it's as if someone's moved them where *they* think things should be, not where we put them. She's bound to have a key.'

'I'll have a word with her.'

'No! No, Phil, you're not to! You don't have to live with her all the time. You don't know what she's like.'

'I think you're getting all this a bit out of proportion, Is.'

'Do you?'

She peered at him over the sheet, her eyes brilliant. How odd the coat looked from this angle, he thought. But it was just a trick of the light.

'I'm keeping it,' Isabel announced. 'She can lump it.

If she's too mean to provide enough blankets in this morgue, what does she expect?'

The word struck Philip in the stomach. But she doesn't know, he thought, it's just a word to her. She has never entered a morgue. *This is our home*, he wanted to protest, but instead he said, 'We're getting those logs at the weekend.'

'I know.'

Her eyes followed him as he put on his jacket and collected his case and coat. She couldn't have looked at him more proudly if he were her well-brushed child, ready to go to school. He stood by the bed, wanting to kiss her, hesitating just too long. He loved to see the curve of Isabel's body in the bed, but the coat blotted her out. She hadn't even tried to get up, make a cup of tea, do anything.

'Goodbye,' he said.

'Will you be late?'

'Probably,' he said, and regretted it as soon as he was in the car.

Chapter Three

When Isabel went out into the hall with her shopping bag, the landlady was already there. Her hair was
bundled in a scarf and she held a bottle of bleach in
her hand, as if she were intending to clean the
cloakroom. Isabel faced her.

'I found a coat in one of the cupboards,' she said.

'What kind of coat would that be?'

The woman must know perfectly well.

'An RAF greatcoat. If it's not in use, I'd like to put
it on our bed. There aren't enough blankets.'

'I've never had any complaint about the blankets,'
said the landlady automatically. Her eyes were avid
on Isabel. The odd thing was that she didn't seem
surprised. She looked satisfied, as if she had eaten
something good.

'Of course, if you need it yourself . . .' said Isabel.

'I don't want it,' said the landlady slowly. 'You're welcome to it. I should have thrown it away years ago. It's nothing but a nuisance to me.'

How could it be a nuisance, thought Isabel in irritation, stuffed away at the back of a cupboard in a flat where you don't even live? Mean old bitch.

'Then we'll use it,' she said aloud.

'You do that, Mrs Carey.' It was the first time the landlady had given Isabel her name. How old she looked today; or not old exactly, but drawn, exhausted. She had done everything to obliterate her looks until she was scarcely a woman at all. Even the shoes she wore were brogues that could have belonged to a man. She rose up from them in a stiff grey column. Perhaps she'd been different when Mr Atkinson was alive. I should feel sorry for her, thought Isabel, but there was still that troubling glint of satisfaction in the landlady's eyes.

'Did you have RAF lodgers here during the war?'

'Why do you ask?'

'Because of the coat.'

'That coat's got nothing to do with anything. They all lived out at the airfield. I should have thought you'd have known that.' The landlady's lips were tight. Why did everything make her so angry?

'It must have been a worry, living so close to the minster during the bombing,' probed Isabel. The great soaring bulk of the minster would have been a prime target for a Baedeker raid. Isabel had already heard that there'd been raids on the town. An airman had been killed on his bicycle, and then the cinema had caught it, but if they were aiming for the minster they had never succeeded in hitting it.

'All that's over and done with,' said the landlady, and Isabel felt herself flush, as if caught out in ignoble curiosity.

She went to the shops. She liked the market, with its rich heaps of vegetables and the freedom to walk from stall to stall, although the stall-keepers' accents were so strong that often she could not make out what they were saying. Consequently she bought in a hurry, almost at random, to get the ordeal over. The other women with their shopping bags and baskets intimidated her. They were so sure of themselves, so sharp and sparing with words. When two or three of them had their heads together, Isabel walked past with her own head held high, certain that they were talking about her. She looked all wrong. Too young, too soft, too southern. Once, a big, foursquare, head-scarved woman rose up to defend Isabel when the fishmonger's assistant picked out for her a partic-ularly limp, dull-eyed pair of herring. 'Now then, Joe, you don't want to go giving her those, it's the new doctor's wife.'

Isabel had not known how to thank her, torn as she was between relief and humiliation. Next time, she swore, she would stand up for herself. She nodded, feeling the colour wash over her face, and the woman said with rough kindness, 'He's not a bad lad, but you want to keep your eyes open.' Girls of twelve knew better than Isabel, when their mothers sent them out with a shopping basket and charge of the purse.

But at the grocer's she was safe. The grocer's wife was a Lancashire woman, eager-tongued and playful, who missed the friendliness of her native county. She was wasted behind the counter, Isabel thought. She could turn a story better than any of the Home Service's stiff raconteurs. It was a quiet day and Isabel gave her order lingeringly. She was the only customer in the shop.

'The town must have been busy during the war, with the RAF.'

'Oh, it was. The airmen all drank at the Red Dragon; it was like the Wild West on a Friday night, and then when they were on ops it was a graveyard. If a crew didn't come back you'd know about it, someone would tell you. They would leave their things in their lockers, you know, before they flew, their private things, and sometimes they'd said beforehand which friend was to have this or that. Watches and suchlike went to the family. It wasn't only the RAF either, there were Poles, Canadians, French and I don't know what else besides. I had a bunch of New Zealanders in here one day, every one of them over six foot. All the girls were after them, but there was more babbies than wedding rings came out of it.'

'And they were here for the duration?'

'Until Hitler threw his cap in.'

A strange excitement rose in Isabel. 'Were there many raids on the town?'

'*Your* house had a near miss. Didn't you know that?'

'No.'

'If you look you can still see the crack in the side, even though it's been filled in. Now then, the boy will be round with your order at six o'clock. He's not been with us long and he's as dim as a Toc H lamp, but he can find the minster, I should hope.'

'My landlady never mentioned that the house had been damaged.'

The grocer's wife gave her a sharp look. 'It was nothing to talk about, compared to what else went on. Besides, she wasn't living there during the war. Not *living*, that's to say . . . She was out at the farm then.'

Isabel found she was leaning forward over the counter, like any gossiping woman. 'I see,' she breathed, willing the other to say more. The figure of the landlady hung in her mind, grey, taciturn, hostile. But perhaps she hadn't always been so—

The shop doorbell tinkled. Two women in battered tweed suits and hats entered, at their ease. Without breaking off their conversation they glanced around for service. Their gaze flicked over Isabel, as vague as it was imperious. No one would try to sell *them* a flabby herring. Instantly, the grocer's wife was with them, inclining her head with a touch of obsequiousness that Isabel hadn't seen in her before.

'Good afternoon, Mrs Huntley-Winterton, Mrs Crosby. How can I help you?'

Isabel was forgotten. She slipped past the women and out of the shop. For a while she walked briskly, as if she had something to do. The houses were packed close together in the narrow streets, and there, at the end, lay the looming bulk of the minster. If she had children, Isabel thought, this is what they would see when they opened their eyes. Kirby Minster would be their native place. But would they ever be at home here?

That night she slept heavily, under the greatcoat. Somewhere in the depths of sleep she heard the phone ringing, and then felt the heave of the bedclothes as

Philip snatched the receiver from its cradle. His voice came at her in waves and then cold air trickled over her body as he got out of bed.

'Phil?'

'Hush. Go back to sleep. I've got to go out to a delivery.'

'D'you wan' tea——'

'Go back to sleep, Is.' His hand was on the covers, pressing them down around her. He liked to think of her curled and warm while he drove out through the deserted town.

It was the coat that pressed her down. She would push it off her in a minute. It was too heavy. But sleep caught her again, melting her limbs, and she was gone deep into the wide skies of Suffolk with the smell of the salt marshes blowing in on the east wind.

'Your parents will be home at Christmas,' said her aunt's voice, firm, practical and utterly to be trusted.

The tapping wove itself into her dream. It was her cousin Charlie, tapping on the underside of the table while she did her maths homework, to annoy her. He had already finished his. Tap, tap, tap, went his fingers, louder and louder.

'Stop it, Charlie,' she said in her dream, but then she looked around and it wasn't Charlie at all, there was a man sitting at the table with her and he had one long fingernail, yellow as bone and hooked over until it was almost double. It was the nail that tapped and the man who looked at her and smiled. Then, very slowly, and so that no one else could see, he winked at her.

Isabel heaved herself out of sleep. She was bolt upright in the bed and her nightie clung to her. Her heart thundered. It was a bad dream, she said to herself, it wasn't real. But in her head her aunt still said, 'Your parents will be home at Christmas,' and the tapping man still winked knowingly. Philip's side of the bed was empty. He must have gone out on a call.

She could still hear the tapping sound that had woken her. It must be her dream still turning, like a record after the needle had been lifted off. Tap, tap, tap. Soft, insistent, determined. It was a real sound. It was coming from the living room. It sounded like someone tapping on glass . . . on a window . . .

Relief flooded her. Philip must have gone out without his key and he was tapping on the front window to attract her attention. He didn't want to rouse the landlady by ringing the bell at this hour.

Isabel snatched up the greatcoat and pulled it around her. Thank heavens he was back. She'd make some tea and he'd tell her about his case and everything would be fine. She ran over the cold lino, into the living room and across to the window, without switching on the light. She drew back the curtains.

There was a man outside the window. She saw the pallor of his face first, as it seemed to bob against the glass, too high up to belong to a man who had his feet on the ground. The street lamp lit him from the side, throwing the sharp shadow of his cap over his face. He was too close, inside the railings that separated the house from the pavement. Of course, the level of the ground there was higher than the level of the floor inside. That was why he seemed to float in mid-air. A man in a greatcoat. An RAF greatcoat, exactly like the one around her shoulders: she couldn't mistake it. An officer. There he was, an everyday figure, safe as houses, but her heart clenched in fear. It was the look on his face: recognition, a familiarity so deep he didn't have to say a word. But she had never seen him before in her life.

He gave her a thumbsup, as if to say, 'Good show. I wasn't sure if you'd heard me tapping.' She stared at him without moving. He was young. Her age, maybe a year or two more.

Her mind struggled from point to point. He thought he knew her but he was a stranger to her. He was on the other side of the glass. He hadn't wanted to ring the doorbell or rouse the house. But he still wasn't Philip.

HELEN DUNMORE

Suddenly, breaking across her thoughts, her body moved. Her arms snatched at the curtains and dragged them across. The man was blotted out. The room was dark. She stood there, clutching the coat to her while the blood banged in her ears. Was he still there on the other side of the glass, waiting? How long had he been tapping before she woke? If only Philip would come home.

But then she reproached herself. Why had she pulled the curtains in his face like that? What a coward she was. He must have lost his way, and wanted directions. There were other airfields not far away, she knew, and some were still operational. The minster was a landmark and it would have been natural to try at a nearby house. Air crew didn't stand on ceremony. They thumbed lifts and whistled at girls. He hadn't meant to frighten her.

Cautiously, Isabel drew back the curtains again. There was no one there. She took a deep breath: of relief, of disappointment, she didn't know. There was the street lamp, shining. Even now, years after the end of the blackout, it seemed like a blessing. She'd grown up in the dark. Isabel pulled the curtains right back, felt for the window-catch and unlocked it. The window slid up easily. She leaned out into the cold night, looked to the right and then to the left, towards the minster. There was no one. The streets were still and the town muffled in sleep. Not a single car was moving. He had rounded the corner and disappeared. She strained for footsteps, but there was nothing.

How good the night air tasted. Cold, fresh and wild, as if the country had blown over the town; but there was no wind. She huddled into the coat and the wool of the collar rubbed her neck. Well, he would find someone to help him, no doubt. There was frost settling on the ground and clinging to the lamp post. The minster roof shone faintly in the moonlight. A man wouldn't choose to walk around for long on a night like this. He would go out to the main road and thumb a lift from a passing lorry, to wherever he was stationed.

She should go back to bed. What if Philip were to come back and find her hanging out of the window, half frozen? In the morning he would say again, in that would-be casual way: 'Is, you are starting to settle down, aren't you? You do like it here?' Or worse, he wouldn't ask. He'd worry over it silently: *Poor old Is, she's letting things get to her.*

She put her hands on the cold sill, ready to draw her head back inside, but a sound arrested her: a vibration, very far off, chafing the air. She listened for a long time but the sound wouldn't come closer and wouldn't define itself. As it faded it pulled at her teasingly, like a memory that she couldn't touch, until the town was silent. Isabel ducked her head inside, pulled down the sash and slipped the window-catch across. Again, she drew the curtains, and this time she felt her way across to the light-switch. The living room sprang out at her in all its dull, ugly banality. What was the time? Ten past three, and Philip was out there somewhere, perhaps at the side of a woman in labour, and so far away from Isabel that she wasn't even in his thoughts.

She ought not to have closed the curtains like that. It was cowardice.

She was still awake when Philip came in.

'What time is it?'

'Half past four.'

He switched on the bedside lamp and sat down heavily.

'Are you all right, Phil?'

'I'm fine.'

'You don't look it.'

'It was a stillbirth. Cord around the neck. Then we damn nearly lost the mother with a haemorrhage.'

'Did you transfer her to York?'

'In the end. You know what those lanes are like. It takes for ever for an ambulance to get down them. Absolute bloody nightmare.'

'It was her first baby, wasn't it?'

'What? Oh. Yes, a first baby. Elderly primagravida in fact.'

'How awful,' said Isabel, thinking of a grey-haired woman straining to give birth to a dead child. 'How old was she?'

'Thirty.'

'Thirty! That's not so old.'

'There's some disagreement over when the term should first be applied,' said Philip with animation. 'There's even a chap who thinks it should start at twenty-six, but he's over in India.'

'It's a vile way of describing anybody.'

'Isabel. It's a precise description which serves a defined medical purpose. That's how we work.'

He was exhausted. He hated to fail. 'I'll make some tea,' said Isabel.

'Don't bother for me. I'm going to sleep.'

He stripped off his clothes as methodically as ever, and piled them on the chair by the bed. She watched his body with pity. In three hours he would be up again, washing, dressing, making ready for the day. He would hate her to pity him. He'd worked so long for all this.

Philip turned to her, socks in hand. 'These need a wash. I didn't know what to say to her. She was lying there and she knew it was dead but no one said anything. She asked me if it was a boy or a girl. I said it was a boy. She said that was what they'd wanted. Then we realised there was a problem with the placenta.'

'You did everything you could.'

He sighed. 'I didn't let her bleed to death, I suppose. What a night. And then there was the husband waiting downstairs. Move that damned coat, Is, and let me lie down.'

It was not the moment to tell him about the officer who had lost his way. Philip fell asleep instantly, without switching off the bedside light. She could see a small shaving cut on the side of his jaw. He must have been in a hurry when he shaved yesterday morning. Already, dark stubble was pushing through his skin. As if he felt her gaze, he twitched and burrowed his face into the pillow, away from her. She lay there for a long time – thinking of nothing, she would have said if anyone had asked. Once she thought she heard a tap at the window in the other room, and tensed, but it was nothing. The light still burned.

'I love you,' she said to Philip's back. It was true, but it sounded false. Instead she said, under her breath, 'You are my husband.' That, also, was true. The word brought back the white gash of celebration that had cut through her life. She had been a bride.

There are some words, Isabel thought, that seem too weighty to be applied to oneself. *Wife. Mother.* But Philip did not seem ever to feel like an imposter in his own life. Perhaps that was why she had married him, she thought; a cold, middle-of-the-night thought she would never have had by day. Towards six o'clock she fell into a sleep so deep that Phil's rising could not wake her.

'Were you warmer, then?' It was the landlady, standing at the top of the stairs, looking down on Isabel.

'What?'

'With that coat.'

'Oh, the coat,' said Isabel, as if it were a thing of slight importance. 'Yes, thank you, it *is* warm. I'm looking out for an eiderdown.' Then, feeling that she'd been ungracious, she added, 'It's beautiful cloth.'

The other woman's wintry face relaxed a little. 'It is,' she said with emphasis. 'Those greatcoats were made to last.'

I could ask you whose it was, thought Isabel. I could ask you why you stuffed it away in a cupboard like that. But I'm not going to give you the satisfaction of denying me the answers. Why should she feel as if she had to propitiate this woman?

'You can't do any harm to it,' said the landlady. 'You sleep with it, if that's what you want, as long as your husband doesn't object.'

'It's not on his side of the bed. He never feels the cold.'

'Men don't, do they? It's as if they have an engine inside them.' The landlady's face was almost animated.

Isabel recoiled. She did not want to discuss men with this woman, or anyone. Still less would she discuss Philip. She should not have said anything about where the coat was laid. It was too intimate: it seemed to allow the landlady into their bedroom. And she's been there, I'm sure of it, Isabel thought. Prying and poking when I'm out. I'm not going to put up with it.

'I must get on,' she said coldly. 'I'm sure you have things to do.'

'It never stops, the work, does it?' answered the landlady, and she continued to stand at the head of the stairs, arms folded, watching Isabel out.

Chapter Four

She would go out to the airfield again. The sky was sleet grey but exhilaration rose in Isabel's blood as she left the town behind. Soon the minster would sink from view. She was alone, and free. She could look through the bare tangle of the hedges into the long ploughed fields, purple and chocolate, stiff with mud and frost. She walked fast, enjoying the strike of her stout heels on the road, and the puff of her breath into the freezing air.

'I must get a job,' she said to herself. She could coach children for their exams. She could give lessons in French conversation. Her accent was good; even French people said so. But Philip hadn't liked the idea when she'd mentioned it to him.

'There's no call for that, Is.' He looked annoyed, almost as if she'd insulted him.

'It would only be a bit of private tutoring.'

'Yes, but – going round to people's houses . . .' He hadn't been able to say what he meant. She couldn't understand what it meant to him, to know that he provided for her and kept her safe. He thought of her going into other people's houses, standing on their doorsteps. He saw her pushing that lock of hair behind her ear, and looking up the street with the little air of remoteness that he loved. They would open their doors and expect service from her. No one else would ever see how beautiful she was. His own mother had thought Isabel was whey-faced and should take iron and drink Bovril every night. As for her hair, why didn't she have a permanent wave instead of all that long slippery stuff hanging down her back, or else pinned up so that strands fell around her face? Not that anything was ever said, of course. That wasn't his mother's way. Hints, slips of the tongue and meaning silences were her style.

I suppose he's worried about people thinking the doctor's wife ought not to work, thought Isabel now. She reached into the hedgerow, pulled out a stick and snapped off the ends. She whipped a stand of desiccated hogweed until the seeds flew.

'You'd make yourself common, Is,' Philip had told her, his face tight.

'*Make myself common!*' She had turned away from him, too angry to speak.

He'd thought, You'd feel different if you'd had to go out in the wind and rain every school night, with other people's groceries on your handlebars. She would never know what that felt like. Even in spite of herself, he would protect her.

How good it was to be away from everything, Isabel thought, swinging her arms as she marched along. The cold stung but she didn't care. She was used to piercing easterlies, those winds that swept clear from Siberia. It was only in the flat that she felt chilled to the bone. But she had escaped from them all: the flat and the landlady's choking presence, the shops and the narrow streets, the looming bulk of the minster, which reared above their dwelling like a totem. She was going back to the airfield even though it frightened her.

This time she didn't hesitate. She walked past the deserted guardhouse and into dereliction. Stronger than ever, the wind buffeted her. Impossible to believe that the airfield had been peopled only seven years ago. Isabel stepped lightly. The roads were broken up and there was mud everywhere. There had always been mud, she remembered, in those wartime winters. The men had lived in it, cycling from Nissen hut to Nissen hut. They needed their bikes, her aunt had said, when a sergeant's tyres were slashed by one of the local boys, outside the Green Man. It was sabotage, said her aunt. It was because of a girl, Charlie told Isabel later.

She wished she had a bike now. She was so small and insignificant, just a dab of life that could be squashed out by a finger. She remembered the vastness of the Lancasters when they lumbered over the sky. Isabel wandered on, past the hangars, drawn as if by a magnet to the main runway. She looked down its length, which disappeared into the distance. No aircraft could land on it now. Maybe time and harsh winters had ploughed up the surface; maybe it had been damaged deliberately, for reasons that Isabel couldn't fathom.

The wind moaned on the perimeter. The feeling of fear was in her again. She had braved it to come here, but still it was stronger than her. It seemed as if she could put out her hand and touch thousands of lives which had never ended but had broken off into a silence that hung more heavily than any noise. They were here, she knew it. The men on their motorbikes who raced the green lanes, or hauled their Lancs into the air with a thunder that made the walls of her childhood bedroom vibrate.

They were not here. They were gone, the survivors back into their lives, the dead wherever the dead go. They would never again ease those huge black machines forward from the dispersal pans, and guide them along the narrow concrete taxiways, onto the chosen runway. She and Charlie had looked up into the air crew's faces, and heard their tales. Not about ops – they never talked about them, and she and Charlie knew better than to ask. But they liked to talk about their Lancs.

The wind blew grit at her and she closed her eyes. It was time to go, and not come back here again. All of it was over and there were good reasons why the place had been abandoned. It was a hostilities-only bomber station, like the one she and Charlie had haunted, pedalling out there on their bikes, getting as close as they could.

She walked away westward. The pall of cloud was breaking up into red streaks of sunset. She turned and saw its reflection pulse at the top of the control tower, where the glass must still be unbroken. Light flashed, and flashed again.

That night Philip wasn't on call. He came home with a bottle of cider and two packets of crisps. Isabel poked the fire until sparks flew and tuned the wireless to the Light Programme. Sure enough, there was dance music.

'But you're tired,' she said, seeing how Philip lay back in his chair. He took a deep draught of cider and smiled at her.

'You can have my salt too,' he said.

Isabel emptied both blue-paper twists of salt into her own bag, held the top and shook hard. She ate her crisps one by one, with slow greed. Philip put down his empty glass and she reached to fill it, but he laid his hand over the top. 'I might be going out later.'

'But you're not on call tonight.'

'No, but the district nurse rang in about an emphysema case.'

'Is Dr Ingoldby ever on call, or does he sit at home holding Janet's wool every single evening?'

'It's all valuable experience, Is. You knew it would be like this.'

'Yes, I knew.'

'Isn't there a play on or something?'

'Don't you like the music?'

'It's all right. If you like it, keep it on.'

It was quarter to ten when the phone rang. Philip leaped up to answer it. She heard his voice through the bedroom doorway, his telephone voice, clear and professional. She heard him take down symptoms and directions. He didn't know his way to the house of every patient in the practice yet, but at this rate he soon would, she thought.

When he was gone she cleared away glasses and crisp packets, and re-stoppered the cider bottle. After a moment's thought she unstoppered it again, poured out another glass and drank it off like medicine. Her head buzzed. She would fall into bed, into the darkest of slumbers where she would think of nothing.

Isabel dreamed of the Lancasters. They came over so low and heavy that it seemed they must lose their grip on the air and plunge down, loaded with bombs, onto the sleeping village. She lay tense, willing them higher. The roof above her was transparent and she stared straight up at the belly of the aircraft that was passing over, and then she could see through metal, too, and there were the men, the pilot like a coal heaver at the controls, the flight engineer alongside him helping to push the throttles forward to get the laden beast into the night sky.

Through the thunder of engines she heard him knocking. This time she knew at once who it was. Her eyes flew open and she grasped the coat to her. He would be at the window in the other room, just as before. This time she wouldn't be a coward. She would go and see what it was he wanted. He must have been drinking in the town, she thought, and lost his way. He needed directions.

In the dark she slid back the curtain again, and there he was. The street lamp lit him and he raised his hand to the window again, but this time he didn't tap on it. He spread out his hand flat on the glass, all the while looking at Isabel. She clutched the coat to her. Her brain was still fogged with the noise of engines. She shook her head, but the sound would not shake out. He was looking at her intently, waiting for something. All at once she understood what it was, and lifted her own left hand, to match his right, and laid it on the glass. They did not quite match, because his hand was broader and longer than hers and so she could still see its outline, seeming to hold her own hand within it. There was nothing between them now but the thinnest possible layer of glass. It felt cold, and then warmer, as if her own body heat were penetrating it. She stood there entranced, and then she saw that his lips were moving. They were forming the shape of her name.

'Is-a-bel. Is-a-bel,' he was saying, though whether aloud or not she couldn't tell. He was on the other side of the glass.

Glass can break, she thought, and fear leaped in her and then died down. She could see that he was not the kind of man to put his fist through a window.

Their hands held still on the glass, and she thought she could feel his heat. At that moment his hand fell. He sketched a brief, humorous salute, turned, climbed easily over the railings and was away down the street. There was another street light on the corner, and as he passed under it his outline showed as clear and sharp as broken glass, before he turned left and disappeared into the shadows.

Isabel let the curtain drop, and pulled it into place. She hadn't realised until now how fast her heart was beating, and she was warm inside the coat, warm as she had never been before in the cold flat.

Now she thought for the first time: How did he know my name? It had seemed quite natural that he should know it, when they were face to face. He could easily have heard Philip calling her, from one room to another. It wasn't hard to find out a person's name.

It was clear to her now that he wasn't a stranger. He was familiar with the area. He must be stationed nearby. He'd come into Kirby Minster for the night and lost his way . . . But surely that couldn't happen twice? It was queer to knock twice at the same window, when you knew no one within the house. And the way he had mouthed her name . . .

The thoughts pattered through her head, logical, sensible, but deep inside her something thrilled like a string under tension. She should be afraid of him, she thought. But how could she be afraid? I won't think about it now, she decided. I'll leave it until tomorrow.

She knew now that she would say nothing to Philip. If she did, he would be furious. He would make enquiries, and call the man a peeping Tom. The RAF officer would not come again. Isabel spread the greatcoat carefully over her side of the bed and crept under it. Everything was quiet now. She huddled down tightly, arms crossed over her breasts, knees drawn up, but not because she was cold. She held herself like someone hiding a secret.

'Who's that? What are you doing? Phil?'

'Hush, Is, I'm bringing in the logs.'

'What?'

The light was on in the living room and through the open door she saw Philip drag a sack to the fireplace. He looked like a hunter bringing home the trussed body of an antelope.

'I've got the logs!' he called softly, triumphant.

'But it's the middle of the night.'

'It's almost seven.'

'And you haven't even been to bed.'

'Don't worry about me. I kipped down for a couple of hours at the Walkers' after I'd got old man Walker comfortable. The oxygen cylinder valve was faulty, that was the problem, but luckily I had another cylinder in the car. He needed ephedrine too – I'll have to have a word with the district nurse – Anyway, young Walker filled up the boot while I was asleep.'

Isabel got out of bed, wrapped her dressing gown around her and went into the kitchen.

'I don't care if you've had two hours' sleep or not, I'm going to cook you some breakfast and then you're going to bed. You can't live like this.'

But she knew already that he wouldn't listen, lit up as he was with fatigue and success. Those dour, word-less farmers had thanked him. He was part of their lives.

She broke eggs into the frying pan and beat them with a wooden spoon while his toast browned under the grill. She would feed him at least, if he wouldn't sleep. Behind her, the logs were already flaring. He'd used fire-lighters, which usually he wouldn't countenance.

'Look at this! They're apple wood, and it's seasoned,' he said. 'They cleared out the old orchard last year.'

His face was eager as a boy's. He was happy with his life, she thought. They wouldn't have had this fire, but for him. Old man Walker would still be gasping for breath if Philip hadn't known what to do for him. It was typical of Philip to carry a spare oxygen cylinder in the car. No, she thought, 'happy' wasn't exactly the word. It was more that Philip belonged in his own life . . . Well, she'd known that before. It had struck her because she so often seemed to be on the outside of her life, looking in, not sure whether she wanted to enter it or not.

'Come and get warm, Is,' he called.

'I'm not cold,' she said, and was surprised to discover that this was true.

'You're always cold.'

She buttered his toast, slid the eggs onto it and carried his plate through to the living room. She saw that he was reluctant to leave his fire, but he went to the table and as soon as he sat down began to wolf the eggs and toast, as if he had just discovered how hungry he was. His eyes were on the textbook which she'd pushed to the side of the table. He always kept a book there so he could absorb information at odd moments. She knew he wanted to pick it up now and make use of the time, but was holding back for her sake. She went over to the fire and spread her hands to the blaze. The smoky sweetness of the wood made her eyes sting.

Philip was already getting up from the table. He would have a strip-wash in the cold cloakroom, a clean shirt, and then he would be on his way to morning surgery.

'I've made your sandwiches. They're in the meat-safe,' she said, rising from the fireside.

'Thanks. What are you up to today, Is?'

'I'm going for coffee with Janet Ingoldby,' she said quickly, to shield her empty day from him, and then wished she hadn't. He might mention it to Dr Ingoldby. 'At least I think I am. But you know how hopeless I am with dates.'

'That's nice.'

'And I'm going to make a steak-and-kidney pudding for tonight. You will be home in time, won't you?'

'Ought to be. Where's my shaving soap, Is?'

'On the chest of drawers. And there's hot water in the kettle.'

When he was gone she would pile the fire high. It wouldn't matter for once. She would make herself busy all day; it would probably take most of it for her to achieve the steak-and-kidney pudding. After that she would measure the chairs and work out how much fabric it would take to re-cover them. She would read a chapter of *Lettres de mon moulin*, to keep her hand in.

By midday, Isabel was deep in flour. She'd rolled out the suet pastry, but it wouldn't make a smooth sheet as it did in the book; it kept crumbling. Perhaps she hadn't used enough suet. Her hair slipped forward and she pushed it back behind her ears.

The doorbell rang. Isabel moved quickly, to forestall the landlady. Mrs Atkinson always tried to answer the flat's doorbell as well as her own. But this time there was no one on the stairs or in the hall. She must be out. Isabel wiped her hands on her apron, unlocked the door and opened it, thinking of the milkman come with his bill, or the grocer's boy with a forgotten item—

But it was him. Of course. She looked at him: his uniform, the shape of him. He was neither smiling nor serious. He looked at ease, as if expected. Yes, she thought, and her hands dropped to her sides. She was open, defenceless. It was him. Who else could it have been?

Chapter Five

He was a tall, fair man, strongly built. He had the Viking look of men from the far north-east. He was not quite smiling at her.

'Aren't you going to let me in?' he asked, and looked beyond her, into the hall. 'There's no one here, is there?' He said 'no one' as if it were a code word for a name they both knew but would not speak. Isabel shook her head. It was true: the house behind her was empty. She was sure the landlady had gone out. Why does he speak to me like that, as if he knows me, she asked herself, not sure if she should feel offence, or fear. But she knew she was neither offended nor afraid.

'I'm all over flour,' she said, in place of the other things that crowded in her head.

She looked down at herself deprecatingly, although

she could tell from his intentness that it was her he saw, not the flour.

'Baking day?' he asked, with a comical lift of his eyebrows, as if she couldn't possibly have any such thing.

'I'm making a steak-and-kidney pudding, but it's the first time, and the pastry's gone wrong.'

'Better not stand around on the doorstep,' he said, glancing behind him.

Of course he shouldn't, she realised. Anyone might see him. She stepped back into the hall, and moved to one side so that he could pass her. Easily, familiarly, he crossed to the door of the flat. She had left it open. It was too late to stop him now, even if she wanted to. He entered, turned to his right, went straight through the living room to the bedroom and sat down on the bed, heavily, hands on knees, head forward, like a man who had run a race. She said nothing. After a moment, he got up again, took off his cap and unbuttoned his greatcoat.

'Fog's worse than this out at the airfield,' he said.

'Oh!' she said. Her thoughts moved strangely, down paths that were foreign and yet entirely familiar. They were paths that had revealed themselves quite suddenly, as if a light had been shone inside her. She was Isabel Carey, and yet these were thoughts that Isabel Carey had never had. She knew what he meant, and she ought not to know it.

'Fog,' she repeated. 'That's good, isn't it? You can get some sleep tonight.'

He shrugged. 'The men want to get on with it. We did an air test first thing to check the starboard inner. Nearly pancaked poor old bloody Katie in a cabbage field, and then ops were scrubbed and we were stood down.' A muscle in his cheek twitched, but he turned it into a smile.

'I'm sure it was a perfect landing,' she said, 'but you do look a bit ropey. Would you like a cup of tea?'

Another smile. 'Haven't you got anything stronger?'

'Wait a minute.' She ran to the sideboard. There was half a bottle of gin left. She poured him a glass and looked at it doubtfully. It was huge.

'Aren't you having a drink?' he asked her, taking his.

'Oh – I don't know. I don't really like gin.'

Again, that comical quirk of his brows. 'Don't you? You could have fooled me.'

She poured a second, smaller measure for herself. He raised his glass to her and threw back the gin. Instantly, he looked better. Isabel took a swallow from her own glass. It was slightly warm: the sideboard was too close to the fire. And oily – greasy, almost. Phil's father had given it to them. His mother had tutted; she didn't believe in spirits, she said. Although how you could fail to believe in something that was real, Isabel didn't know.

'Have another,' she said, proffering the bottle. She felt so much at ease. Maybe it was the effect of the gin, but it seemed perfectly natural to have a man in RAF uniform drinking with her in the middle of the day. The question of where he was stationed and what he was doing here could be sorted out later.

'Aren't you going to take off that apron?'

'I've got to finish the pudding.' There was flour on the rim of their glasses, where she'd touched them. She wiped her hands on the apron, and poured out his second drink. 'Let me take your coat,' she said, as if he had just arrived, an invited guest.

His coat, when he handed it to her, was warm. She folded its bulk and laid it on the bedroom chair. He was taking off his boots. With a sudden movement he threw himself down on the bed, full-length, staring up at the ceiling.

'You don't know how good this feels,' he said, and then he was silent, lost in thought. 'To be indoors, in a proper house, not those bloody huts. When I was a kid I used to wish they'd let me sleep outside.'

'In a tent, you mean?'

'I wanted them to pull my bed out under the stars. I'd have my sheets and blankets and Mum's eiderdown, and a hot water bottle if it was snowing – and I'd let the snow fall on my face. You know when you look up into a snowstorm it's like looking into a tunnel and the flakes go round and round inside it?'

'Did it ever happen?'

'Not likely. Now I shouldn't care if I never went outside in my life. Come over here and lie down.'

'I told you, I'm covered in flour.'

'It's only your apron.'

'And my hands.'

'I don't care. They're *your* hands.' Already his eyes were half shut. She saw how deadbeat he was. Marked, weary skin. He smelled of cigarettes, sweat, metal, the soap he'd scrubbed himself with before he came to her.

'Filthy night,' he murmured.

'Did you get much sleep?'

He shook his head from side to side, slowly, luxuriously. 'Three hours. This pillow smells of you.'

She was at the top of an endless slide, clinging to the rail, looking down at the fall. He was a stranger, but she knew him. Every word he spoke and every shadow of his expression fitted patterns she had never seen before but which had always been there, beneath the skin of her life.

'Who are you?' she breathed. Instantly, his eyes flew open and he gave her a brief, brilliant smile, as if they shared a joke. Philip is much more handsome, she thought. But this man was looking into her face, her eyes, as if they knew each other so well they didn't have anything to explain. They could be silent if they chose. He was utterly exhausted. In the fog of her mind a name was forming: his name. Soon it would be close enough to pull it to her, like a handle to open a door.

She stepped backwards. Her heart thudded in her throat. He had flung his right arm up and his face was perfectly still, as if sleep had caught him in the middle of a breath. She kept backing away, through the door, into the kitchen where her suet pastry still lay on the table. She lifted the saucepan off the gas and peered inside. The meat had cooked too long, and the gravy was as sticky as toffee. Isabel turned off the gas, untied her apron and brushed the flour off it, over the sink. She had placed a tiny mirror there and her face stared back at her, pale and startled, with bright eyes. She bit her lip, hard, until it hurt and the skin went white. It was real, then. She was this person, Isabel Carey. On the wall the little clock, which Philip had rescued from his dad's Jowett before it was scrapped, said ten to eleven. Isabel watched the clock for a full minute, to be sure that time was moving, and then she left the kitchen.

He was still there. Fast asleep, deadbeat. No wonder, she thought, and then checked herself. Why was it no wonder? But she knew. Everywhere she looked, more of his life appeared from the shadows.

Charlie used to let her watch while he developed film in his improvised darkroom under the stairs. First there was nothing and then the detail swam into view as he lifted the negative in triumph from its bath of fluid and hung it up to dry. All she had to do was look.

Isabel kicked off her shoes and lay down on the bed beside the man, on top of the covers. He gave out heat steadily, like an engine, while his weight pressed the mattress down. He was heavier than Philip. At the thought of Philip a pulse of alarm went through her, and then vanished. He was out for the day at least. He'd be miles away. She thought of Philip's profile, as she'd often turned to watch it while he was driving. She could study every inch of him because he so rarely felt her gaze and turned to her.

The man's greatcoat lay folded on the chair, but her greatcoat, *the* greatcoat, was no longer there. A thin counterpane covered the blankets, as it had done when Isabel and Philip first moved into the flat. Isabel was lying on top of the bedclothes but she wasn't cold. There he was, on Philip's side of the bed, next to her, on his back. She put out her hand and touched his shoulder. The fine wool of his uniform was pleasant against her skin. She felt as if she'd known its touch for a long time. Here they were, the two of them. He'd been outside for a long time, but now he was here in her bed. She thought of the tapping at the window that had broken into her dreams. Maybe, on other nights, he had tapped and she hadn't heard. He had been waiting for far too long. *I shouldn't care if I never went outside in my life,* he'd said. Philip was different. He grumbled sometimes when the telephone rang and he was called out, but he liked it too. He would whistle under his breath as he fastened his collar, because the world needed him.

It was as quiet as those days when snow begins with a few desultory flakes and then thickens, thickens until the sky is full of it, muffling streets, cars, houses, footsteps. Isabel had moved a little closer to the man in uniform. Her body seemed to know how to curve itself to his heat. She was quite safe: she knew he wouldn't wake. She would let him have his sleep.

Time went by. Intently and silently, time fed on the peace of the bedroom. Isabel was asleep.

She woke at three. It was already dusk outside the window. No, it was fog, wrapping itself around the lilac that grew in the backyard, close to the window. Branches pressed up to the glass, dripping wet.

There was nobody beside her. Isabel passed her hand over the bedclothes and thought she detected his warmth, but it might have been the heat of her own body. Perhaps he had made a hollow in the bed; but then the mattress was so old that it went naturally into peaks and valleys. With a swift movement she rolled over and pressed her face to the pillow where he had laid his head. Yes, he was still there. Cigarettes; a smell of engines; something men put on their hair. The greatcoat was lying in its usual place on top of the bedclothes.

Isabel swung her legs over, got up and went to the kitchen. The important thing was to finish making the steak-and-kidney pudding. She tied on her apron and as she did so she heard the landlady's footsteps overhead. *She must have come home while I was asleep.* All the way to the window Mrs Atkinson walked, went back to the door, and then to the window again. The usual tread, too heavy to be ignored. Isabel switched on the radio, tuned it to the Light Programme and turned the volume up high on *Music While You Work.* Harry Leader's sax soon took care of the footsteps. Isabel hummed along loudly as she poured a cup of hot water into the sticky gravy, stirred it and set the pan back on the hob. She rolled out the pastry again and this time it held together, flaccid but obedient. The recipe text danced: *Grease the basin . . . line the basin . . . pour in prepared meat and gravy . . . cover and seal . . .*

She did it all. She was a young married woman in her own kitchen, listening to the radio as she prepared her husband's meal. No one, watching her, could imagine anything different. *Pour boiling water into a large saucepan, place prepared pudding basin on the trivet, cover, leaving the lid askew. Steam for two and a half hours, adding more boiling water at intervals.*

By then he would be home. It would be Philip sitting opposite her, no one else. He would praise the pudding, no matter how it tasted, because she had made it.

The door to the bedroom was ajar. What a ridiculous arrangement it was, to have the kitchen off the bedroom. It was the way the house had been divided; she supposed that once it had all made sense, when it was whole. It annoyed her, the way things got broken up so that they couldn't fit together properly any more.

If you lay on the bed and the door was open, you could watch someone who was standing at the stove. She refused to turn. He was there again, she was sure of it. He had come back without her hearing him. He was still lying on the bed, but he was awake now, and refreshed. Some colour had returned to his face. His arms were folded behind his head and he was watching her.

His name was Alec. She knew it now. It had come

into her mind as she slept beside him, as if he had whispered it into her ear.

'Alec,' she said, turning. As she'd thought, he was there. His eyes were narrowed, to watch her more closely. They were dark blue; navy, almost.

'What?' he said.

Suddenly a low vibration turned into sound. He moved his head sharply. It was the same heavy sound she had heard before, coming closer. The deep thrumming of four Merlin engines as the aircraft came low, ready for landing. She and Charlie used to identify them when they were miles away, before the adults could hear them. A Lanc.

Alec was sitting bolt upright. His expression had changed completely: he was preoccupied, anxious, charged for action. He swung himself off the bed and came to her. He stood very close – too close – and again she was afraid.

'Alec,' she said, 'what is it?'

'I've got to go.'

'But you haven't said—'

'Said what?'

'You haven't told me your surname.'

His face held nothing for a second but blank astonishment. 'What are you talking about, Is? What's the matter with you?'

'Your surname,' she insisted.

'What is this, some kind of a game? You've been a bit queer all day.' He cupped her cheek with his hand, and at that moment she discovered that she knew it, of course she did, how could she have asked Alec such a stupid question?

'Sorry. It's probably the gin,' she said. His touch was so intimate that it gave her gooseflesh.

'I've got to go,' he repeated.

'I know.'

His boots were on, and his greatcoat wrapped around him. He set his cap on his head, and he was gone. She heard the door bang, and ran out into the hall after him, pulled open the front door and looked right and left up the street. There was no one. The fog pushed towards her, and she shivered. You couldn't even see the minster clearly. How would the Lanc ever land safely? As she thought this, she realised that the noise of its engines was fading. Fading, and then gone.

Chapter Six

He'll come back, she thought. It wasn't speculation: she was sure of it. How could he not? The flat still breathed his presence, even though it was Philip who sat opposite her, eating the steak-and-kidney pudding. He praised it, as if she were a clever child, and told her that it was as good as his mother used to make.

'I should think so,' said Isabel, having endured his mother's meals.

'Did you have a nice time with Janet Ingoldby?'

'What?'

'You went for coffee with Janet Ingoldby.' Again that note of patience in his voice. She was shrinking in his eyes, she thought, while the rest of his life expanded.

'Oh . . . No, I'd got the day wrong. It's next week,

I think. Just as well, really, because I had a lot of shopping to do and it took hours to make the pudding. I'm fearfully slow.'

'You'll get quicker.'

'Will I?' she asked. To her amazement, he was perfectly serious. He didn't want her to tutor local children in French. He didn't want her going into other people's houses, earning money and using her qualifications. He wanted her to learn to cook. He was so handsome, she thought. His face remained dark, remote, romantic, even while he chewed the tough meat and thought about his patients. He was in his own world. He'll have to be careful, thought Isabel. Some of those patients will fall in love with him. They'll start inventing illnesses, so that they can see him, and he won't know why. He'll tell me that they are hypochondriacs.

She considered him. You might say he was modest, and praise him for it . . . But had anyone got the right to be so unaware of his effect on others?

Philip ate quickly, fastidiously. Isabel knew he wanted to get to his desk. There would be something niggling him – a symptom he wasn't quite sure about, or a diagnosis he was beginning to doubt. Soon he'd have his books piled around him like a fortress, over which she might hand him a cup of tea. He would glance up at her with that sweet but absent smile.

She hadn't known anything about marriage. Her father and mother had vanished while they were still the sun and moon of her world. Her uncle had been away for the whole of the war, and when he returned after fighting his way from North Africa to the north of Italy, it was clear that he and her aunt barely knew each other. The trim, youthful figure who had been on parade on the mantelpiece for six years had become a grey-haired man who lost his temper easily and couldn't stand noise. She and Charlie quickly learned to keep out of his way. As soon as he was old enough, Charlie had cleared off to the other side of the world.

But Isabel knew Philip. She had been sure of him. The formalities of the wedding were a thorny thicket that they had to hack through in order to be where they wanted. And they'd done it. Private, ruthless exhilaration had gripped them both as they drove away from the church in his father's car, on their way to the three days in the Peak District that would be their honeymoon. The figures of his parents dwindled behind them. His mother had already turned to clear away the remains of the wedding breakfast. Aunt Jean staunchly kept on waving, having fulfilled to the letter every detail of her duty and affection to her niece. Philip and Isabel were on their own, and it was all about to begin. It seemed incredible that somehow they had robbed the bank of happiness and now they could spend their treasure as they liked, over the days and years to come. Philip drove, while Isabel sat beside him, watching the road unfurl. From time to time she glanced at his profile, or lit a cigarette for him and put it between his lips. That was in June. It was no time ago, and yet everything had changed.

'That was very nice,' said Philip, putting down his knife and fork.

'Good,' she said, taking his plate. There would be more, and better, steak-and-kidney puddings. There would be processions of meals. She would meet more Janet Ingoldbys, with their efficient knitting, their children away at school, their gardens and their good works. Rivers of coffee would be drunk, and mountains of little cakes would be popped, one by one, into the mouths of women gathered to chat. They would soon accept Isabel as one of themselves.

'Any interesting cases today?' she asked brightly, as she cleared the table.

'Are you all right, Is?'

'What do you mean?'

'Oh, I don't know. You seem a bit down.'

'It says in *Early Days* that the young wife may take time to adjust, after the excitement of the wedding is over.'

He thought of their wedding, with Isabel in a blue linen dress and coat, clutching a bunch of crimson roses as if they might escape. Her dark, slippery hair swung down, touching the petals. She'd refused to have it waved, or to wear white, or have any fuss.

'I can't ask Charlie to come all the way back from Australia to give me away,' she'd said. Philip believed that she wanted a quiet wedding because of her parents. It was understandable. Isabel's mother should be sitting in the front pew, between smiles and tears, while Isabel's father walked her proudly up the aisle. If they were not there, why go through with the whole performance? The quiet wedding suited Philip well enough, never mind if it didn't please his mother. To be married to Isabel was all he cared about.

'Come here,' he said.

'I've got to do the washing-up.'

'It can wait—'

'Just listen to her! That bloody woman! It's like living with a gaoler.'

The landlady was walking again.

'She hasn't enough to do, that's what it is,' said Philip.

'No, it's not, can't you see? She's doing it on purpose. She knows it drives me mad.'

'Why, have you said something to her?' he asked in alarm.

'Of course I haven't. But anyone would know, if they were marching up and down on top of other people. *Can't* we get somewhere else, Phil?'

'We'd lose money. We paid three months' rent in advance. We've got to save every penny or we'll never have our own house.' He wasn't taking her seriously. His handsome face was worried, but only because she was upset. 'Forget about her, Is. Let's go to bed early and get a good night's sleep for once.'

Isabel didn't seem to hear him. 'Why would anyone walk like that,' she said, as if to herself, 'Unless she had a bad conscience?' Maybe the landlady wasn't a gaoler. She might be a prisoner. Prisoners walked like that, pacing their cells, so many steps one way and so many steps the other, until they could walk it in their sleep. 'Perhaps that's what it is, Philip!'

'What?'

'Perhaps she sleepwalks. She goes on all night sometimes – haven't you heard her?'

'No. Besides, somnambulism is much rarer than people imagine.'

In bed that night Isabel lay stiffly on her side of the mattress. Philip had rolled off her and fallen deeply asleep. Her thighs were sticky, and cold. But I'll never have a baby, as long as we stay here, she thought. It was as if the landlady's spirit was everywhere, in the fabric of the house and in the waves of sound that beat against Isabel's eardrums. Philip said he couldn't hear it, but she didn't believe him. He was trying to pretend that there was nothing wrong.

The darkness of the bedroom brushed against her wide-open eyes. Of course it was not really dark. After a while, the bulk of the chest of drawers and wardrobe shouldered out and became visible. She thought of the blackout, and how there was complete darkness then, pushing itself into mouth, eyes and ears. She remembered hearing footsteps behind her in the blackout when she was walking home. Suddenly she'd realised that they were keeping time with her own. She stopped, and the footsteps stopped too. There was a breathing, waiting silence. She realised that the man was waiting to hear her again, so that he could follow her. Silently, she stooped and took off her shoes. She'd walked on silently, on tiptoe in her stockinged feet, not daring to run.

The bedroom hung over her, heavy and permanent. They'd come here so lightly, full of their own happiness, setting up camp, accepting that it would do for the time being. They'd both believed that it didn't really matter what the place was like, because it was temporary. They were on their way elsewhere.

Perhaps people always have to think that, Isabel thought. For an instant she allowed herself to think of the places where a woman might end up. She saw her mother's face, unrecognisable, in the landscape that Isabel had pieced together from newsreel and newspaper articles, after the war in Japan ended. She saw skin and bones, shovelled into a grave that wasn't deep enough.

'Don't think of that,' Isabel whispered savagely to herself. She forced her mind to clear, but her mother came again. This time she was leaning out of the train window, with Isabel's father behind her. The guard had blown his whistle, and with heavy chuffs the train had begun to move. It was very slow at first, and Isabel could easily keep up with it as she pulled her hand out of her aunt's grasp and began to run alongside the carriage. Her mother wasn't waving. She stared intently into Isabel's face. Isabel ran faster, wreathed in the train's smoke, hearing her aunt call out behind her. The train was moving faster now and her mother's face became a pale disc with dark hair blowing around it. Now Isabel seemed to be running backwards as the last carriage overtook her, and her mother was gone. Isabel was at the very end of the platform, out in the sunshine. There was fireweed growing beside the track. She looked back, and in the darkness under the station canopy, there were Aunt

Jean and Charlie. Aunt Jean said something, and Charlie began to run towards Isabel.

That woman; that damned woman. She was walking again, with venomously light tread, as if she could judge to a nicety exactly how much noise would keep Isabel awake, without disturbing Philip. She knew that Isabel was lying on the other side of the floor, helpless to avoid her. We'll never get away, thought Isabel. *She'll* make sure of that.

But she could rebel. In one sweep she was out of the bed, gathering round her body not her own dressing gown, but the greatcoat. She tiptoed over the lino, into the living room, and silently through to the door that opened into the hall.

There was the moon, in the fanlight over the front door. Following her own moon-shadow, Isabel crept upstairs. She had never been upstairs to the landlady's floor, not once. Mrs Atkinson had always come down to them. There was a cheap wooden door, put in when the house was converted, Isabel supposed. Behind it were the landlady's quarters, and the stairs to the attics. Isabel could see that the wooden door opened outwards. She raised her fist and rapped hard with her knuckles.

The house went still, listening. The footsteps

stopped. Isabel waited. After a few seconds, she heard footsteps again, this time coming towards the door. There was the sound of a bolt being drawn back, and then a key in the lock.

Isabel slid back against the wall, close to the door's hinges. She spread herself out until she was only a deeper darkness within the darkness of the landing. She barely breathed.

The door was flung open. Isabel put out her hand and caught the brass of the Yale latch so that the door would not rebound from her body. As it opened, it hid her.

'Is it you?' came the landlady's voice, oddly eager, oddly young. Isabel heard her take a step forward, out onto the landing. 'Is it you? Where are you?'

She was at the banisters, looking down into the hall. Isabel moved sideways a fraction. But it was not the landlady at all. She must have a guest staying with her. No wonder the voice had sounded so different. This woman was young. She leaned forward so that her hair swung and shone in the moonlight, and called again into the well of the hall, 'Is it you?'

Isabel did not move. After a minute the woman turned. Now she had her back to the moon, and there wasn't enough light for Isabel to see her face. Her head was bowed. She walked back to the flat's entrance and pulled the door shut behind her. Isabel heard the snick of the lock, and then the bolt sliding across.

The landing and hall still quivered with the words the woman had called out so eagerly, but in soft, cautious tones, as if afraid somebody might overhear. *Is it you? Where are you?* It was a younger and sweeter voice than the landlady's, but the accent was the same, and the voices bore a family resemblance. Even the shape of the slender body that leaned over the banisters wasn't entirely strange. The landlady must have a young relation staying with her. A niece, perhaps.

Isabel waited, in case someone was listening and waiting on the other side of the door. There were no more footsteps. As silently as she had come, she tiptoed down the stairs and back into the flat.

Philip was still sleeping. Isabel spread out the greatcoat and lay down under it. A strong, subtle electricity filled her, and she knew she wouldn't be able to sleep. She could have walked for miles down moonlit lanes, all the way to the airfield. Her heart throbbed, but not with fear. It was Alec. He was gone, but he still possessed her thoughts, charging them, making her tingle from head to foot. Wherever he was, she knew that he was hungry for her. When Philip lay on top of her, smiling down into her eyes, Alec was there too. He'd watched, standing at some distance from the bed with his arms folded. Those dark-blue, almost navy eyes of his had seen so much that they could be surprised at nothing. His face was still young, but not his eyes.

Chapter Seven

Each night, Isabel tucked the greatcoat around her, before she fell asleep with her back to Philip. Alec came in the afternoons, or late at night when Philip was out on call. He never stayed long. Sometimes it was a bare minute, sometimes half an hour. He tapped on the window. When she opened the house to him he would enter like a sleepwalker, unsmiling, so weary he could barely speak until he'd had the first drink. Sometimes he sat on the bed, knees apart, head bowed, hands on knees, as he'd done the first time.

Soon she understood that it took him this time to come back to himself, when he came to her straight from a debriefing. The racket of the Lanc was still going through him, as if he'd been welded to the throttles and couldn't disengage. She saw the vibration in his fingers. She stepped forward and put a glass into his hand. Sometimes he had a beer, but more often it was gin, because that worked more quickly. The gin jumped in the glass and then he swallowed it down and everything began to level off.

After the first couple of days, she realised that she would have to be careful. Philip had noticed the level going down in the gin bottle. It worried him that Isabel didn't go out more. As far as he could tell from the descriptions she gave of her days, they seemed to consist of shopping, walks and cooking. Whenever he suggested something she might do, or join, she evaded him.

When Philip had first known Isabel, he'd loved to watch her read. He would see a smile flicker across her face when she got to a passage that amused her, and hear her sigh as she tucked her feet under her and turned the page. But her French novel had lain open at the same place for days. He couldn't read French, but he could read page numbers. What did she do with herself all day?

'Cleaning and cooking,' she said.

'You could get a charlady,' he said, trying out a word he'd heard other people use. His mother had cleaned every inch of the house herself. 'We can afford it.'

'I don't want anyone here!'

'It would make life easier for you.'

'It's bad enough, the way everyone watches me in the shops.'

She spoke sharply, in a new way. She looked different, too. A little thinner, he thought, but not ill. In fact she looked marvellous. During his training, he'd come across doctors who drank and hid it. But what on earth would Isabel be doing with a bottle of gin? Pouring herself a glass with her lunchtime sandwich? He couldn't picture it. But there was the evidence. He would raise it with her tactfully.

Isabel laughed at him – a real laugh, which made him realise he hadn't heard her laugh for days. She told him it was his imagination. So there was the fact of the gin bottle, and there was Isabel laughing with bright eyes and clean breath. He wasn't going to pursue it. He would believe her.

The next day, Isabel took a train to York and bought another bottle of Gordon's. It was too risky to buy spirits in Kirby Minster, in an off-licence where someone might recognise her. In York, she was free. Ordinarily she would have spent the whole day in the city, wandering the narrow streets, visiting shops and the museum in blissful anonymity, but she was afraid to stay away from the flat for too long. She thought of Alec tapping at the window. With the gin wrapped in brown paper at the bottom of her shopping bag, she took the next train home. Cunningly, she poured half an inch of gin into the old gin bottle, and then the next day half an inch more. From now on, each time the level sank, she would restore it.

She'd caught Philip with the gin bottle in his hand, holding it up to the light. Instantly, she knew how stupid it had been to try and fool him. He was far too precise for that. *She* might have accepted, vaguely, that the level in a bottle might come and go: never Philip. He turned to her and his eyes had a hot, hurt look in them, as if he'd caught her out in behaviour that violated his idea of her. Suddenly she was afraid of what he might look like, if he ever knew that she had deceived him. A man like Philip . . .

'Do I look like a secret drinker?' she asked, trying to make light of it. He regarded her. His gaze travelled over her skin, her eyes, her hair, in the way she had loved when they were courting.

'No,' he said flatly, 'you don't. You look very well.'

She was lit up from inside, and she couldn't hide it. Her eyes glowed and her pale skin was flushed. He looked at her and she looked back at him: neither yielded. They were two separate people, intolerably close.

In bed that night he said suddenly, 'Isabel.'

'What?' she asked drowsily, although she was wide awake.

'There's nothing wrong, is there?'

'No.' She lay very still, waiting, but she didn't think he had fallen asleep. He was waiting, like her. The landlady, for once, must be sleeping. The bleak, dreary darkness of the flat seemed to gather itself like a blanket over their bed. I don't want to be here, she thought fiercely. I've got to get away.

'Philip?'

Nothing.

'Philip?' she said again, a little louder.

Still no reply, but he was awake, she was sure of it. She listened to his steady breathing, and for an instant she hated him with all her heart, because he was allowing her to fall like this, away from him. *Very convenient,* said a cold little voice inside her. *Blame your husband, why don't you?*

Isabel never asked Alec where he was stationed. When he mentioned the airfield she nodded as if she knew it well. It might have been any one of the dozens all over the east of England. He had a motorbike, he said, and one day when it was warmer he would take her for a ride on it. They would ride out to the coast.

'If you won't be afraid.'

'No, I shan't be afraid.'

'Have you ridden pillion before?'

HELEN DUNMORE

She shook her head.

'You'll be fine. All you have to do is hang on to me.'

But another afternoon he said to her, 'We'll have to get out on the old bike again, Is. You remember those geese?'

She smiled but did not answer. In her mind a skein of geese flew with steady wingbeats, from east to west. She'd seen them many times, on their migrations. Now she saw herself too, with Alec, raised up on a bank at the edge of a marshy field. They shaded their eyes against the sunset as they tracked the flight of the geese. At first it was like watching a film, but as she watched it the images entered her and became part of her. They were Isabel's memories now. She was no longer quite certain of what had really happened. *Had* she been out on the bike with Alec? How long had he been coming to the house? In a clear, lit part of her mind she remembered the first time, the knocking on the window, her own cowardice, and then how she'd had sight of him on the other side of the glass. But the rest of her mind was filling with memories that came from somewhere outside her own life. They were crowding in and there was only that small, lit point, always growing smaller, to tell her that they were not her own. It was because of Alec. He was doing it. Or was it? She didn't know. Philip . . . she clenched her hands and dug her nails in. She would hurt herself and break the dream. She would think of Philip. Yes, she could do it if she wanted, she could still fill her mind with her husband: there he was, his dark, carved profile, the lift of his chin. But even when she summoned him up, he wouldn't turn to her. He didn't even know she was there. He had pretended to be asleep! He couldn't help her now.

Alec was smiling at her. She gave way and let the surge of those other memories enter her, and become her.

'Yes,' she said, 'the geese. That was a good day, wasn't it?'

'Promise me you'll come out on the old bike again?'

'Of course.'

'She may be clapped out, but she really goes,' he said. All at once his smile faded. He released her and stepped back. 'What time is it?'

She looked down at her wrist but she wasn't wearing her watch. 'Hang on.' She went into the kitchen to look at the old car clock, and called back, 'It's all right, Alec, you've got plenty of time.'

He didn't answer. Even as she turned, she knew he'd already gone. There was his glass, there was his cigarette on the edge of the ashtray, still smouldering. Her hands twisted in frustration. What was he playing at?

* * *

After a while Isabel grew calmer. She was getting used to it, she supposed. Alec was staying for longer each time, she was quite sure of that. After that long first visit, his time with her had shrunk to seconds, then grown again to minutes. Today, they'd had half an hour at least. How could he stay longer? He had to get back to the airfield. She thought of all the bits of time that Alec had spent in the flat. If only it were possible to sweep them together, and see what shape they made. Sometimes it seemed to her that it was the same day, over and over.

Alec barely touched her. She put her hand over his and its trembling grew worse, but after a while it stopped. She longed to walk towards him as he came in from the hall, unbuttoning his greatcoat. She wanted to press herself into him, inside the coat, so that it would enfold them both. Then, she thought, they would be together. But he was too quick for her, and it never happened. Each time, he walked straight through to the bedroom. Each time, she took his greatcoat, folded it and laid it on the bedroom chair.

She offered him food, but he was never hungry. He said he'd be having his pre-op meal later. 'Eggs and bacon. Does that make your mouth water?' he asked her teasingly. 'What are you having – snoek pie?' He wouldn't even take a slice of the sponge cake she'd baked for Philip. He drank gin, and sometimes a half-pint mug of tea, and he smoked cigarette after cigarette.

Sometimes, in the early days, he would be gone after the first drink and cigarette. But one afternoon she understood that she should sit down on the bed beside him, and put her arm around him as he stared down at his knees. He smiled without look-ing at her, and leaned his head sideways until it rested on her shoulder. It was a swift movement and so full of intimacy that she did not know how to respond. But it was only for a second and then he was back in position, looking down, deep in thought. Then he took her hand, weighed it, rocked it within his own. She felt the heat of his body, burning into hers.

It was the next day that they went out to the airfield. She was washing a jumper when the doorbell rang. It was a cold, bright day and the wintry sun dazzled her as she opened the door. There he was, and there was the motorbike behind him, propped against the kerb. He didn't seem to care about anyone seeing him today. He was wearing his flying jacket, a leather helmet with a strap under his chin, and goggles pushed up on top of his head.

'I've borrowed some clobber for you from Syd,' he

said, and held out a second, smaller jacket and leather helmet.

'That skirt's no good,' he said, looking at her, 'and I couldn't get Syd to part with his trousers. What else have you got?'

She was ready in ten minutes, dressed in a pair of tartan trews she'd had since she was sixteen, with Philip's heaviest winter trousers over them and rolled up. Syd's jacket was warm, and almost fitted her.

'Irvin jacket, airman, for the use of,' said Alec.

'Syd must be small.'

'He's a midget. Just as well – you want a rear gunner who'll fit in the turret.'

'I suppose you do,' said Isabel.

She was sitting behind Alec, with her arms around his waist. Her feet were on the footrests.

'We'll go as far as the airfield,' he said. 'There isn't time to go to the coast today. Not too cold?'

She shook her head as he glanced back over his shoulder. He looked quite different out of doors. Younger, as if a heavy weight had slid off him. He loved the bike, she could see that. He seemed to think she already knew how to ride pillion, so she didn't ask questions. It would be easy enough to hold on to him.

'Remember that time I got her up to seventy-five?'

'Not today,' she said firmly.

'Not with you on the back, any day.'

At that moment two women rounded the corner. They were Janet Ingoldby and a younger woman whom Isabel didn't know. They were deep in conversation, walking slowly, heads close. For a second Isabel felt a pang. This woman, her face warm with friendship, was a Janet Ingoldby she didn't know. Immediately, the thought was pushed away by fear. Janet mustn't see her. She would recognise Isabel, even in this get-up. She would see her on the back of a motorbike, with her arms around Alec's waist, and Dr Ingoldby would hear about it, and then Philip – at that moment, Janet Ingoldby raised her head and looked directly at Isabel. She was smiling as she made some point to her companion. In fact, she was pointing; pointing at Isabel's house, saying something Isabel couldn't quite hear. She had looked straight past the motorbike and the two people on it. Isabel ducked her head down to hide her face. She saw nothing now but the grain of Alec's jacket. He kicked down on the starter and the engine fired. The vibration went through Isabel and she held close to him. Janet Ingoldby would never see her now. As they rode off she risked a backward glance. Neither woman was looking her way. The noise of the bike hadn't disturbed them at all.

Once they were out of town, Alec opened the throttle. The bike leaped forward, bare hedges rushed at her, the earth tipped as the bike took the bends in the lane. She was drowning in the noise of the engine. She had no choice but to mould her body against Alec's and try to lean into the bends. But she was afraid. She could sense her own fear pouring through her and into Alec, breaking the bond between them. He couldn't ride if she sat stiff like this. She heard a noise in her own throat, a gasp or a protest. He was uncertain too now. She felt the bike slow and he turned again, taking his eyes off the road to glance at her. It was going to end in failure. He was going to know she didn't belong here, on the back of his motorbike, in the middle of . . .

He was going to find her out.

No. That mustn't happen. Isabel breathed out, long and slow. There was nothing to fear. The lane curved to the left and she gave way to it, so close to Alec that there was no room for anything to go wrong between them. As he leaned, so she leaned. They were one creature with the same noise and vibration going through them both. The bike came up. They were out of the bend, back on the straight. She moved a little so that she could see over his shoulder. The white lane flew towards them, overgrown where it had once been wide enough for two trucks to pass at speed. Alec opened the throttle and they went faster.

She wanted to go on, past the airfield and all the way to the coast, but she felt the bike slowing. He was right; there wouldn't be time. She saw him raise his right hand, greeting someone she couldn't see.

The broken fence stretched out ahead of them. At the entrance to the airfield, the guardhouse guarded nothing. She could see everything that was invisible to him, although it was a quarter of a mile distant: blackened weeds, split concrete, gaps where the wind blew. Alec pulled over by a gate at the entrance to a farm track.

'I'd be pushing it if I tried to get you through the guardhouse,' he said. He stripped off his gloves. 'Are you frozen, darling?'

The word went through her. Philip never used endearments. She was Is, or Isabel; he hadn't been brought up to sweetheart a woman, and she understood that to him it was both unnatural and unnecessary. They were married. They lived together. He entered her body. That was the reality, not words.

It was strange to think of Philip but find him still so distant, as if he lived in another world. Or as if he were lost in a fog. Yes, that was it. One of those fogs that rolled in from the east, with the smell of the sea in it, in spite of the distance. Such a fog would quickly cover everything.

Alec was sharp, and close. He was standing by the leafless hedge, lighting a cigarette. She watched the smoke and drew in the scent of tobacco. Around his mouth there were grooved lines, too deep for so young a man. In the bottom of the hedge, a thrush rustled and then was still. She saw the bead of its eye, watching them.

'What can you see?' she asked, talking to the bird. She couldn't deceive herself any more. Perhaps the bird saw a woman on her own, on a winter's after-noon, talking to herself. Perhaps it saw nothing. Alec hadn't noticed that Isabel had spoken. He was unlatching the gate.

'Come on,' he said urgently. He pushed open the gate for her and they went through it, picking off thorns from last year's brambles. She stepped care-fully over the ridges of the plough, following Alec. A track, very faint, like a long abandoned footpath, ran to the next corner, where there was a broken-down stile. Alec climbed onto it, and held out his hand to pull her up. He seemed not to see that the wood was rotten. It held under her weight, and he caught her hands as she jumped down.

She saw now where he was heading. There was a hut in the corner of the next field. Maybe it had been a shelter once, but now the door hung open and the corrugated iron roof was eaten away by rust. He was leading her towards it. Even in winter, the hut was hidden from the road by the hedge and steep bank. From here you could not even imagine the airfield. There could be nothing for miles but fields in their winter slumber, their ploughed earth hardened by last night's frost. It was very still.

'Here,' he said, and stood aside as if holding open the door for her, even though it hung off its hinges. She ducked and went into the hut.

The air seemed warmer inside. There was something soft underfoot. Alec came inside too and there was light from the doorway. The floor here was also rotten, and the old carpet that had once covered it had sunk into the pulp of the wood, so that it seemed to be woven into it. The carpet had been red.

It was dry enough inside, and smelled of earth. There'd be spiders and beetles, but there was no reason for rats to settle here.

'Here we are,' said Alec. She saw that he was smiling. There was so little space inside the hut that they stood together awkwardly. A shadow passed over his face. He glanced around quickly. Suddenly, naked fear seemed to possess him. Isabel backed towards the door, but he put out his hand and held her.

'Don't go,' he murmured rapidly, 'Don't go, Issy. It's quite safe. I've got plenty of time.'

'But what's the matter?'

'I couldn't see the mattress. I thought someone must have moved it.' She knew at once that he had seen what she saw: the carpet rotted into the rotting wood, rust and decay. But he was strong. 'It's all right,' he said, pointing down, 'there it is. Mattress, Alec and Issy, for the use of. Must have been a trick of the light. My God, the things you see, when you've been staring into the dark for hours . . . When they send up a scarecrow you think it's some other poor bastard's kite . . . '

'It's all right, Alec,' she said. There was no mattress.

'I'll spread out my greatcoat. You'll be as warm as toast.'

'But you haven't got your greatcoat . . .'

She looked, and saw that he had it, over his arm. He spread it out carefully over the floor, and then he folded up his long legs, sat down and smiled up at her. She had never looked down on him before. He seemed so much younger. His fair hair sprang thickly from the crown of his head. She put out her hand to touch it, and again he caught hold of her.

'Come here. Come on, Issy, we haven't got much time.'

Of course they hadn't. She understood it as well as he did: no, not understood but knew. There were no miles of empty, fertile fields beyond the hut. There was a bare half-mile before the airfield began. As she sat down beside him, he was already taking off his jacket.

For a moment Philip moved in her mind like a ghost. He was walking away to the car, case in hand. A miniature Isabel trotted at his side. Now they were driving together, two small creatures on their way to a destination Isabel no longer remembered.

It was too cold to take off their clothes and even Alec couldn't see any blankets. They clutched each other through wool and cotton, pushing aside fabric until they touched skin. She put her lips on his bare neck and pressed into the warmth of him. He tasted of salt and cotton, Lifebuoy soap, cigarettes and engine oil. She nuzzled him with teeth and tongue, taking him in.

It was soft underneath her, as if they were lying on a mattress. She felt the prickle of the greatcoat as he pulled away her clothes to touch her. He smiled and touched her cheek as if there was all the time in the world but then they were caught up and shaking together, all lips and mouths, spit and wet hair trailing across her face, and then she was opening herself to him wider than she had ever known, and he was in her, part of her, so deep she forgot everything.

Chapter Eight

There was a place for his head between her chin and her breast. They lay for a long time like that, slowly returning to themselves. Perhaps they'd been asleep for a while. His hair was dark at the roots with sweat and his face was huddled against her. He must have got engine oil from the bike onto his hands and then run them through his hair, for she could smell the oil, and something else, like cordite after a firework explosion. He had twisted a length of her hair through the fingers of his left hand. When she stirred, it tugged like an anchor.

I must go home, she thought, I'll be late.

Home . . . But where was home? Her mind struggled in a darkness that was new to it. It was as if Alec had entered her mind as well as her body, taken her and left himself there. He had possessed her.

Possession, she thought, and her mind shivered for an instant in terror. But no, he was warm and breathing, as warm as she was. She would not think of anything different. They belonged together. Time had cracked, and given them to each other.

She shifted position, moving carefully so as not to disturb him. There was nothing in the world she wanted more than for him to stay there, where he was, against her. Her thighs were sticky. He'd come inside her and she'd held him tight, not wanting him to withdraw even though she knew they should be careful.

Home . . . But instead of the drab rooms of the flat, a grey stone farmhouse filled her mind. Its image developed. There was a line of washing blowing on the green, to one side of the house. The back door was half open and she found that she knew what lay inside. She knew the kitchen with the range that had to be black-leaded until it shone. Her fingers had learned the exact pressure to put on the cloth as she buffed up the surface. There was the Dutch airer that came down from the ceiling on thin twisted red-and-cream ropes. She knew how it swung, and how she had to loop the rope around the hook while she was hanging up the clothes, so that the rope would not pay out suddenly and dump the rack full of clean washing on the floor. In winter, the clean clothes smelled of her cooking. She didn't mind baking smells, but she didn't like it when her blouses reeked of roast meat.

As Isabel watched, the kitchen stopped being empty. Shadowy figures were starting to form, drifting like smoke at first and then spinning themselves into solidity. She snatched her mind away. They would dissolve if she didn't look at them. Above all she didn't want to see their faces. A sense of terrible urgency seized her and she shook Alec awake.

'Alec! Alec! I must go home. Look at the time.'

He rolled over, away from her, and lay on his back bewildered, collecting his thoughts.

'What's the matter, Issy?'

'I can't be late. He'll get worried.' *Worried* was code. It meant suspicious.

'I thought you said he was going to York with his brother?'

'No,' said Isabel. Alec's words moved in her head, making no sense. 'I never said that. He hasn't got—'

'Stay a bit longer,' he said, reaching out for her. His eyes were as open to her as the sky. 'Don't go yet, sweetheart.' Again his endearment moved her, melted her, but she scrambled to her knees, fastened her clothes and brushed them down with her hands. There was a strong, musky smell of sex. She smoothed her hair, knotted it at the nape of her neck and reached into her pocket for her handkerchief. She spat on the cotton and wiped around her eyes and mouth. Alec was dressing swiftly. He stopped, and said to her, 'Do my face too.'

'You're fine. It doesn't need it.'

'Go on.'

She spat on the handkerchief again and wiped around his mouth, and then wiped his forehead. He was right: his face wasn't clean. There was a film of grime on the cotton now, as if engine oil had sweated from the pores of his skin. But his skin was so fair and close-textured – so sweet to her touch . . .

'Your handkerchief smells nice,' he said.

'I keep lavender in my handkerchief drawer,' she said, and saw herself in a garden she didn't know, snipping flowers off hoary lavender bushes, to dry them. Tentatively, she followed the memory further. There she was, coming indoors with a basket full of lavender. As she reached the green paint of the back door she saw that the sun had blistered it, and it was beginning to crack. But there was nothing to be done about that. It was impossible to get paint these days. She pulled the door open with her foot and then pushed it wider with her hip, because she hadn't a free hand.

Now she remembered back to her first meeting with Alec. It was all coming clear, as the flat and

Philip grew cloudier and more distant. These were that other one's memories, and now they were hers, too. The farmhouse; her life there; the woman she'd been. Geoff had met Alec in the pub, got talking about cricket, and asked him over for high tea on Sunday. There was a cottage loaf, their own honey and an apple cake. Geoff had told her Alec was from Newcastle, and he'd been been over in Canada on the Air Training Plan. Canada! she'd thought. The furthest she'd ever been was York.

She'd always loved a Geordie voice. There was no more than a trace of it in Alec, but it was there. He was an educated man, an officer. He'd liked the baby. He had put his hand down into the basket where he slept, and stroked the baby's cheek, awkwardly, as if he wasn't used to babies. A pang went through her. He looked up, smiled, and she saw how his eyes were dark blue, almost navy. He was a big man, bigger than Geoff, but his touch on the baby's cheek was so light that William didn't stir. She had to drop her eyes.

She put the heavy teapot on the table, and began to slice the loaf. She could sense him watching her. She poured the tea.

'I suppose you'll go home, when you get leave,' she said, for she wasn't going to ask him if he was married. Most of them weren't, she knew; they were too young.

How old would he be – twenty-two, twenty-three? But they always looked older than they were.

'That's reet, canny lass,' he'd answered softly, teasing her. She'd given a little gasp, as if she had a stitch. Geoff was supping his tea noisily, and didn't hear.

Isabel caught her breath. What she was remembering did not belong to her. I am Isabel Carey, she told herself. I live in Kirby Minster. My husband is a doctor and his name is Philip Carey. She muttered the words to herself like a spell, and Alec, the Alec of now, heard her. He glanced at her, she shook her head, deprecating herself, and he turned back to doing up his bootlaces. Now he was whistling under his breath. It caught at her, how content he looked, and she found she was smiling too. He looked up.

'What is it?' he asked.

'Nothing.'

'You were smiling.'

'I like watching you when you're doing something like tying your laces. You know how you can be quite close to someone – and yet there are expressions of his that you'll never see? When he's working, or on his own in a train compartment.' She was thinking of Philip. He was sharp in her mind again. She saw him tracking across the countryside, uncovering it lane by lane, on his own and not even thinking of her.

'Only quite close?' Alec asked teasingly, but she had Philip in her mind and she stared without understanding. 'I'd have said we were closer than that.' He looked into her eyes boldly. Philip would never do that. For him, what they did in bed was a world apart from their daytime selves.

'*Very* close,' she said, with a swagger to match Alec's, letting her naked self appear in her face. Why had she let herself think of Philip now? She must push him away. It wasn't safe to have the two of them together in her mind: Philip and Alec.

Suddenly Alec's smile disappeared. His attention switched from her. He was frowning, preoccupied. 'It can't be late,' he said, as if to convince himself.

'It might be. It's ridiculous, neither of us wearing a watch.'

She could hardly believe he'd been so careless. He had to have his watch with him. It had to be accurate to the minute. He was the Skipper. A minute – a second, even – might be a life. He'd told her that they all synchronised their watches at the end of the briefing.

Alec was looking at his wrist, where the watch should be. There was a paler strip of skin where the strap usually covered it. She looked at the beauty of his wrist, the way it turned, the springing hairs that were darker than the fair hair on his head. She felt as if the blood were leaving her face, a backwards tide taking her life with it. She had got to touch him, have him—

'Can't think what happened to it,' he said. 'Must be in the hut.'

He meant the long Nissen hut where they slept, with one iron stove to heat it. He had his slip of a single room, because he was an officer. He had his iron bed, his locker, his table, the muddy walk to ablutions. It was one hell of a way. You'd spend half the day walking if you didn't have a pushbike. These hostilities-only bomber stations were all the same. Nothing but mud, barbed wire, concrete and corrugated iron. Temporary cities thrown up in the middle of cabbage fields.

'It'd better ruddy well be there. If I've dropped it in the mud— '

'It'll be by your bed,' said Isabel.

He glanced uneasily over his shoulder, at the white glare of the winter afternoon.

'Better get a move on. I can take you back on the bike, Issy.'

She fastened Syd's jacket and put on the helmet as they crossed the fields to the lane. Now she felt bolder. She was Alec's girl, who rode pillion on his bike. But as they came out of the hut, Isabel heard the sound that had haunted her childhood: a Lanc's engines — Merlin engines. An engine caught, then roared into life. And then the next, and then the next, and then the next. Port outer, port inner, starboard inner, starboard outer. The engines roared at full throttle, then the sound eased and died back.

'That'll be N-Nora,' said Alec.

'You can't know that!'

'She's had repairs to the port outer. They're testing,' he explained, as if to a child, but she saw that he was already more than half over the border into his own country beyond the wire, in the engine noise, knowing what every reverberation meant. The intensity of his listening seemed to pull the sound towards them.

'You've got to go,' she said, before he could say it.

'Yes.'

But he stood irresolute, his eyes on her. She realised that he was waiting for something, and then she knew what it was; nothing high-flown, just the jacket he'd borrowed for her from one of his crew. 'You'll need this,' she said, stripping off Syd's jacket. 'Here.' She was already pulling off the leather helmet.

'You won't be cold?'

There was something graceless in the way he asked the question, as if it didn't much matter whether she was cold or not. She was suddenly not quite real to him. Isabel shivered with the sudden lifting-off of the warm sheepskin lining, and with the sense of her own self suddenly ghost-like. Alec's mind must be elsewhere; surely he wouldn't leave her like this otherwise, in the middle of nowhere, without a coat. 'Feel how thick my jumper is,' she said, wanting to make something better of it than the reality. 'I'll be warm as toast. I'll go back across the fields.'

Alec folded the jacket, tucked the helmet inside and strapped it to the carrying rack. 'You sure?'

'Sure.'

He swung himself onto his motorbike and kicked down on the starter. He was leaving. She reached out, and touched the leather of his jacket, as if for luck, but he didn't notice. As the bike moved forward he gave her a thumbs-up, and then the wheels spun in the dry mud and he was gone.

The roar of his bike vanished instantly, as if cut off. Wintry quiet enveloped her. Dry leaves rustled where they had drifted at the foot of the hedge, and the same thrush hopped through the undergrowth. She'd need to get going. She had to walk back to town, and by the time she got there it would be dusk.

But Isabel did not turn in the direction of the town. Instead, she walked the other way, towards the airfield. She had to see it again.

There was no sound of aircraft. No vehicles

passed her. The lane was narrow and overgrown. She walked steadily, keeping her eyes down until she had rounded the lane's curve and knew that if she looked up she would be able to see the broken wire and the huge emptiness of the airfield.

She heard an engine behind her. Almost as soon as she heard it, the lorry was on her. It swept past with its canvas-covered load, so close that it grazed her sleeve. The driver didn't even sound his horn. She jumped back, and as she did so a second lorry passed, and then a third. She waited, pressed against the hedge, while the convoy passed. There must have been ten lorries. She saw their drivers' faces, tired and indifferent, pushing on. The smell of exhaust gripped her throat. She was trembling. The lorries had ploughed past as if she were nothing. The men didn't glance at her.

But still she was drawn onwards, towards the perimeter fence. Suddenly the air filled with sound, as if someone had turned up the volume switch on a radio which had been playing, muted, all the while. She heard engines, and, above the noise of the engines, she heard voices.

The guardhouse roof was intact. Figures in uniform moved around it. Lorries were passing through the gate, one by one, stopping by the guardhouse for the driver to show his papers, and then moving on.

She looked along the perimeter fence. It was perfect. The airfield's buildings were complete. There it lay, a hastily built city with its temporary air hardened by use. She scanned the low curves of Nissen huts, the brick admin block, the control tower with tiny figures visible through the unbroken glass windows. Somewhere there would be a bomb store, camouflaged against air attack. Charlie knew all the names of the bombs, and how heavy a load the Lancaster could carry in its bomb bay. Tallboy, Wallis bouncing bomb, cookies and Grand Slams. As the bombers lumbered above their heads, climbing, Charlie would guess at where they were going and what they were carrying, just as if he'd been in the briefing with the crew who were now passing above them, and had seen the chart with its routes marked by tape.

In the distance, a tractor hauled a long train of bomb trolleys. She shaded her eyes and stared into the hangar opposite her. Through the dazzle of winter light she thought she saw the shadow of a Lanc, with ground crew swarming over it. Must be serious damage, she thought, or they'd do the repairs out at dispersal.

Isabel closed her eyes. Waves of sound beat against her ears: the noise of a hive, full of purpose, humming with its own life. Alec was in there somewhere.

He would smell of Isabel, as she smelled of him. If she was real then he was real too.

She and Charlie had both known the outlines of aircraft. They'd fought to be first to identify each one as it flew overhead. Once, only once, it had been a Junkers 88, in broad daylight, coming in so low that a ploughman had said in the pub, 'I saw his dom face.'

Now she opened her eyes and saw the face of the airfield. It was here. It was not a ghost, or if it was one, then she was too. It had imprinted itself too deep for time to wipe the landscape clean. The air crew cycling from mess to barracks would be glad of the dry weather. Even so, there was mud wherever she looked, and she saw how it would deepen and become a sea as winter wore on, and then it would freeze, and thaw, and freeze again. The mud would be there, churned by boots and wheels, until spring came. The mud would outlive the men.

'Alec,' she said under her breath. The sky was loud with the noise of Merlin engines. She moved forward until she was pressing her hands to the fence, but no one turned or appeared to see her. The wind blew harder, and the windsock by the taxiway closest to her filled with it and pointed at Isabel. It seemed to be the only thing that knew she was here.

Her body ached from the wind. It was so cold; she couldn't remember ever being so cold. Why had she told Alec she would be warm? The wind penetrated her. She was raw to the bone and yet she couldn't leave. She had to watch them. A couple of ground crew walked past her, along the perimeter track. One of them whistled tunelessly in the teeth of the wind. The other talked animatedly, as if to himself, about a football game. His words trailed past Isabel in snatches. His boots, striking the concrete, were clodded with mud.

They were gone. The fence dissolved and Isabel clutched at nothing. There was the control tower with its windows broken and obscenities scrawled on the brick. She saw that the corrugated iron roof of the guardhouse had rusted. Every soul had vanished, as if blown away by the wind. But they were still there, she knew that. It was only that, at this moment, she couldn't see them.

Alec was at her side.

'I've been waiting for you,' he said. 'I had to see you.'

'Waiting for me? But you can't have been – you've only just this minute left me.'

'Listen. Ops are on for tonight. Briefing's at four. Nothing's been said but the gen is we're off to the big city again. Listen, Issy. I'll come to you straight after the debrief. It's only quarter of an hour on the bike. I'll knock on your window. Swear you won't go to sleep.'

'I never go to sleep. But be careful on the bike — you won't have slept — you'll be so tired—'

'There's no traffic at that time.'

'You'll be all right, Alec.'

'I know I shall. Only four more ops to go, counting tonight. Four's got to be a lucky number — four-leaved clover, remember? — Besides which I've got your knickers, air crew, for the protection of.'

She laughed. He had stolen her pre-war silk knickers, the ones she kept for best because you couldn't get anything like them these days. Except that there wasn't any 'best' with Geoff and so they'd been hidden away in the back of her drawer, until Alec came. Geoff thought that women who wore fancy underwear were whores.

The knickers went with him on every op. He wouldn't let her wash them. She pretended to be shocked, but she knew it meant there was nothing of her that he didn't want. She hadn't known it was possible for a man and woman to be like this. His crew thought Alec's silk gloves were their mascot, and he let them believe it. How tired he looked, she thought. Sucked dry. The bones in his face were sharp. He was due leave again in ten days' time, but the crew didn't want leave. All they wanted now was to finish the tour. They wanted it so much that it was like possession. Once Alec had let his guard down and talked of the future: what they might do. He'd be screened for six months at least after the tour. They'd meet in York or Lincoln, depending on where he was posted. They'd get a hotel room. They'd find a way. Those places were full of wives coming to join men on leave. They'd be just another couple.

He only talked about it once. It was bad luck to talk about the future. No, that wasn't it, not exactly. He'd tried to explain to her. He had to be 100 per cent here, now, there couldn't be any part of him that was absent. He had so much in his mind – all his training, all his experience, those nights when you either came back or you didn't, and if you did you came back with new, sharp, hot fragments of knowledge. It all had to fit together. It had to be remembered instant by instant. He had to hold it all in his mind, so that it wasn't even like thinking any more, it was all there without him having to think about it. And then his mind was free to do the other things, beyond his training, that might keep them alive. It was that freedom which made him faster by a fraction of a second when Syd's voice banged through the intercom: 'Corkscrew port go go go—'

She thought he looked exhausted. No, he told her, he wasn't finished yet, not by a long way.

'You're not getting rid of me that easily,' he said.

Then he was silent, frowning. She knew from his face that there was something more he wanted to say.

'What is it?' she asked.

'It's Rod,' he said. 'He's not so good.'

'What's the matter?'

He shrugged. 'It's nothing. These bloody stand-downs are getting on everyone's nerves.'

He was silent again. He'd told her once that there was another look you saw sometimes. When you saw it you didn't say anything. Just glanced away again and kept on putting your clobber into your locker or whatever else you were doing. The chop look. She'd asked him what it was. He'd said there was no other word for it: it was what it was. Crew had it when they weren't going to come back. They didn't know it, but something in them did and if you were unlucky you glimpsed it.

'The chop look,' she'd repeated, her face twisting as if she'd tasted something foul.

'That's it. But I'm telling you, you'll never bloody see it on my crew.'

He had never mentioned it again. Now he said, as if he were arguing with someone, 'He's a bloody fine wireless op, though.' She put her arms around him and leaned into his chest. Now the wind had to blow past them, because there was no space left between them.

'You shouldn't be here. You should go home, Issy,' he said in her ear, but she knew he didn't want her to leave him.

'*You* shouldn't be here,' she answered, 'I don't know how you got off the airfield.'

For the first time she sensed the outline of something within him, like a vulturous shadow leaping between them. It flapped there in huge distortion, then he folded it into himself again and crammed it down. No, she thought, not distortion. It was real.

She remembered the words her mother had said long ago, when she had perched on Isabel's bed to comfort her for a day of troubles that ended in soaked, helpless crying. Her mother had said, 'Don't cry, darling. It will all look different in the morning.' She could remember her mother's words but not what had come next. Had Isabel stopped crying? Or maybe it had never happened, any of it. Her mother had been gone for so long that Isabel was beginning not to know where memory ended and making her up began.

It will all look different in the morning. Nothing worse could be said. He knew what had to happen before there was morning for him. She held him close. She knew the odds too but they couldn't apply to Alec. He was so much here and so much himself; *present,* as they used to say at school when the register was called. How could someone be present and then ripped out of life in a few hours' time? But there was nothing easier. He knew it, and he'd made her know it.

The night-fighters would come in from underneath to attack the belly of the Lanc on the inward run when she was bombed up. That's why you had to keep weaving, so the rear-gunner had a chance of spotting them. Last week they were waiting for the bomber stream over the Dutch coast, beneath thin cloud cover. They got a Lanc on his port side, two hundred feet below. It came at him in a ball of light. Pulse after pulse of explosion rocked them. There was no plane, no men, no parachutes, no nothing. Already he was corkscrewing. Syd's voice on the intercom, more peevish than anything: 'Fuck it I've gone blind.' Metal rattled on the fuselage – flak or Lanc debris, he didn't know. He was up to altitude again and he hauled her into the second dive. When they levelled out there was Syd's voice in his ear, back to normal, as if nothing had happened, 'Keep weaving, Skipper.'

A shard of metal had smashed the Perspex and Syd had been cut across the head, which filled his eyes with blood. It took him half a minute to realise he had to wipe it away. Later Laney crawled back with a bandage. They took the mickey out of Syd for days: *Fuck it I've gone blind.*

He told her these things and she kept them in her mind. When she heard the engines starting up across the fields she listened. She heard them on the taxiways and she heard them take off but she made a blank of the time between take-off and landing. When she could, she left the farmhouse, went into town and waited for Alec there.

'If I don't look after the lodgers, they'll give notice,' she told Geoff. He didn't argue. It was good money the lodgers paid. She'd hired a girl to look after William, on the strength of it.

The other one's memories swarmed in her head, and then they faded. She was Isabel again. Alec pushed her away from him and looked into her face. She wondered what he saw.

'I'll knock on the window. Listen out for me. You remember that day when you wore Syd's jacket?' he asked, as if it were long ago.

'Of course I remember.'

'As soon as this is over, we'll go to the coast,' he said. 'You and me on the old bike. I know a place where we can go.'

'I'd like that,' she said. Time swung and then righted itself. How long ago was it really, since they were together in the hut? To her, it seemed no time at all. He had been with her, he had gone, he had come straight back to her. But to him, it was part of their shared history.

It didn't matter. It could be as long ago as he wanted. She was wasting time, struggling to understand things in a way that wasn't Alec's. It didn't make any difference. He was here, and soon he wouldn't be. A minute could be a year, if it would take that look off his face.

'Just think, Issy, if it could always be like it was in the hut, when we didn't have our watches. As if there wasn't any time.'

'But if there wasn't any time, then I'd never be able to see you.'

He shook his head, smiling as if he knew something she did not. 'If there wasn't any time, then you would always be able to see me,' he said. 'You still don't understand, do you? I'll always come to you.' He gave her another gentle push. 'You've got to go, or they'll find me here with a popsy when I should be in the briefing room. They'd take a very dim view of that. *LMF, old boy.*'

The rims of his eyelids were red. 'LMF?' she asked.

'Lack of moral fibre, sweetheart. Gets you carted off to scrub bogs in the back end of beyond. They make sure we know all about LMF.' He pushed her away again, this time almost angrily.

'You don't have to do that,' she said, holding his eyes. 'It's me, remember?'

He sighed, and pulled her back to him. 'I know. I'm sorry, sweetheart. I'll see you in the morning.' His voice was sure but his eyes stared past her into the dusky winter afternoon. 'It gets dark so early now,' he said.

'Yes,' she said. She leaned up and kissed him quickly, by the ear, so that she could not taste him too deeply, want him again, pull him to her and never let him go.

Around them the airfield spread out in dereliction. 'Look, Alec,' she said. How much she wanted him to see that everything he feared had ceased to exist. There were no more ops to be flown. There were no Lancs to fly them. The dispersals were empty. The concrete runways and taxiways were broken up and full of weeds. It was all over.

He was looking, but she didn't know what he saw.

'*Look*,' she insisted, but instead he caught her in a close, fierce embrace and she felt herself melting, her mind changing. Again she saw the grey farmhouse, her home, and the green door. Out of sight, a baby was crying, on and on. *My baby*. Isabel jerked herself away from him. '*Look!*' she told him, taking it all in with a sweep of her arm.

'You know what, Issy, I'm going to try and slip you

past the guardhouse,' he replied instead. Now they were walking arm in arm, towards the wide-open entrance. There were brown tufts of last summer's grass. He propelled her ahead of him through the desertion.

'There's no one on guard,' she said.

'The boys owe me a few favours,' he answered.

They were through, inside the airfield. Alec walked briskly.

'We're going to the mess,' he said.

He knew it was impossible. He knew as well as she did that he could never get her past the guardhouse and into the mess. Even wives had to live an hour's drive from the airfield. He knew it, and so, she guessed, this time he must also see the dereliction that permitted it. He must know that there was no one to challenge him.

They went into the mess, pushing aside the door which hung off its hinges. Others had been here before them. Sections of the lino had been cut up and taken away. There were no tables.

The bar was still there. Alec leaned against it, taking a handful of coins from his pocket. She stared around as he rapped on the counter and ordered their drinks.

'Not a bad band,' he said. 'We'll dance, shall we, when you've finished your drink?'

She watched dead leaves scuffling over the floor. All the windows were broken, and it was as cold in here as it was outside. It smelled of musty earth. Alec stood with her, calm, untroubled by the fact that they had no drinks in their hands. After a while he said, 'Shall we dance?'

They revolved for a while, to music Isabel couldn't hear. It was easy enough to follow his lead as he steered her expertly, to avoid the other dancers. After a few minutes, he let go of her. He looked around, his face knitting with anguished bewilderment. She did not even dare, this time, to ask herself what he saw. She dropped her eyes as he struggled to regain his calm.

'Sorry, darling,' he said at last, 'I must press on. Can you find your own way home?'

'Of course,' she said.

Chapter Nine

Isabel cut the cake and put a slice on Philip's plate.

'You've been busy,' he said.

'Yes.' She poured more tea for both of them and sat back. She was so tired. She yawned, stretching her arms and twisting her shoulders luxuriously as a shudder of fatigue went through her.

'Early bed tonight,' said Philip. He was getting this clipped way of talking to her. She supposed it came from keeping his surgeries to time when patients grew loquacious. How they must yearn to talk, stuck out on those lonely farms . . . She shuddered again and her eyes watered.

'I'll make some fresh tea,' she said, getting up, but she stole a look at Philip over her shoulder as she went to the kitchen. He was bent over his slice of cake, cutting it absorbedly. She saw the dark sweep of his lashes. 'No man should have eyelashes like that,' she'd said to him the second time they went out. Or perhaps it was the third . . . He'd been surprised. He'd laughed awkwardly, as if he wasn't sure it was a compliment, and she'd felt awkward too. The subject had lapsed. She'd understood then that you couldn't tell a man to his face that he was handsome. There'd been other awkward moments before Isabel had learned what Philip liked her to say and what he didn't. She was too impulsive. He liked her to be calm.

What if she turned back to him now and said, 'Here's your tea. I spent this afternoon in a hut in the middle of the fields, with another man.'?

'Isabel has a great deal of imagination,' one of her school reports had said. 'She must take care to distinguish between fact and fiction.' Aunt Jean had frowned over that. She said nothing, but Isabel knew she'd been branded as a liar. The injustice of that report burned in her for years.

'I've got something for you,' Philip called through.

'What is it?'

'Leave all that. Come and have a look.'

He led her through the front door, down the steps and to the car. The street was cold and dark, but when he opened the boot there was enough light from the street lamp for her to see a parcel filling the space, wrapped in brown paper and tied with string. Philip took it out. 'Here you are,' he said, and laid it in her arms. It was soft and light. She looked over the bulk of it at Philip, smiling thanks, but at that moment she saw, beyond him, the landlady. Mrs Atkinson stood there with one hand on the railing and one foot on the bottom step. She was watching Isabel and Philip intently.

Isabel had been on the point of pulling off the string to open the parcel, but now she said to Philip, 'Let's go inside.' She raised her voice, so the landlady would hear her, and, sure enough, Mrs Atkinson went quickly up the steps and vanished inside the front door. Philip had noticed none of this.

'All right,' he said, a little disappointed. He had liked her eagerness to open his present.

Isabel glanced up the staircase as they came in, but no one was there. Just the usual dank smell of polish, Jeyes Fluid and old food. It seemed so everyday, but she knew it wasn't so. The house had tricked her before and it wanted to trick her again. She had the sense of a held breath. Something – or someone – was hungry. Their hunger wanted to grip Isabel and pull her in.

'Lock the door, Philip,' she said when they were back in the flat. 'I left it on the latch.'

But the landlady had a key. What if Philip were to

fix a bolt on the inside of their door? Isabel knelt by the hearth with the parcel. Carefully, she undid the string, rolled it up and unfolded the paper. Philip stood by, looking down on her as if she were a child opening her Christmas presents under the tree. A puffy mass of silk swelled out of the wrapping. It was an eiderdown, covered in roses and trellises of leaves.

'I thought it would keep you warm,' he said.

The eiderdown expanded, pushing itself free. 'Where did you find it?'

'I had to go all the way to York,' he said proudly.

'You were in York today?'

'Yes. I had to tell you a white lie, I'm afraid, Is, when I said I'd be out making calls.'

'*Oh . . .* Did you go on your own?'

'What an extraordinary question. Of course I did. Who on earth would I go with to buy an eiderdown?'

'Fancy you having a secret.'

'A nice secret, I hope. I had to order it. You won't be cold now.'

'No.' She folded the eiderdown carefully, lifted it, and took it through to their bedroom. It billowed, unwieldy, as she spread it out. The roses were bigger and redder than any rose she'd ever seen. They rioted over the bed.

'It looks very cosy,' said Philip from the door.

'Yes, it does. It was very clever of you, Phil. Thank you.'

It was hideous. She could smoke in bed and set fire to it, perhaps.

'I'll leave you in a bed of roses in the mornings,' he said, rather sentimentally. Philip never talked like this – what had come over him? Isabel busied herself with tucking in the sheets and patting everything smooth. But it was no good. Her hands hated the silky, insinuating touch of the eiderdown. She stood up and said, 'There's a good play on the wireless tonight. Let's listen in.'

'Have you noticed something?' he asked.

'What?'

'She's gone quiet. Her upstairs,' he said humorously, jerking his head in the direction of the ceiling.

'But you said you couldn't hear her.'

'Once or twice; nobody could help it. But there hasn't been a peep out of her for days. At night, I mean.'

'I hadn't noticed,' said Isabel.

'We'll be out of here soon,' he said in a rush, as if he were making her a promise.

'I know we will.'

'It'll be just the two of us then. There'll be no one to interfere.'

She looked at him sharply, but his face was

innocent of suspicion. All he meant was that they wouldn't have to answer to a landlady once they had a place of their own.

The whole weight of the house seemed to press down on her. She was afraid again. Alec's words echoed in her head, but now they were more than a promise: I'll knock on the window. Swear you won't go to sleep. She saw his eyes on her. Her heart clenched at the remembered expression on his face. He was outside in the dark and the wind, staring in at the warm, lit world. Whatever happened, she knew that Alec would come for her, and she would slip into that other life again, her mind clouded with memories that weren't hers, her body moving to rhythms it had learned elsewhere. Nothing on earth could stop him from coming, or her from becoming that other woman, once he was there. There was no one strong enough to hold her back.

If she told Philip, he'd think she was mad. That would be dangerous. Philip would have the medical profession on his side if he decided that she needed treatment. She could imagine how his face would change. He wouldn't see her as Isabel any more, his wife, the one he loved. His expression would be a doctor's, full of concern and impersonal pity.

He could have her locked away. She knew what that meant. She and Charlie used to watch the crocodile of inmates from Burleigh Hospital, on the rare occasions when they were allowed out of the grounds. Women as old as her aunt wore ankle socks, clumsy sandals and shapeless cotton print dresses, with no belts. They looked like big, deformed children. Her aunt had said, 'They used not to let them out at all. Perhaps it was kinder that way.'

Or, worse, Philip might think: Isabel has behaved like a tart and now she's trying to get round me by pretending to be a madwoman.

A shutter would come down and he would never trust her again. She knew him well enough to understand that it wasn't a question of forgiveness; he wouldn't be able to bear the sight of her.

'Yes,' she said aloud, 'just the two of us.'

It was too warm under the eiderdown. She longed to push it off, but didn't dare. The dark hours wore on. There was a wind that spattered rain on the bedroom window. The house creaked under its buffeting, but Philip didn't stir. Upstairs, too, it was silent. The greatcoat, folded up by Philip, lay on the bedroom chair. She was safe under Philip's eiderdown, but she lay there rigid with effort, struggling against the desire prickling in her limbs. She longed to creep out of bed, snatch up the greatcoat and cradle it in her arms like a living thing, before spreading it out on her side of the bed and waiting, waiting . . .

'I won't,' she whispered. 'I won't. I won't.'

Nothing answered. The room was quite indifferent.

In the morning she had a headache. Philip brought her tea and aspirin, and perched for a minute on her side of the bed, stroking back her hair. His eagerness to be on his way, and the husbandly decency that made him remain, were both so palpable that a smile crept onto Isabel's lips.

'What's so funny?'

'You are. Go on. Where are you off to today? Another of your secret trips?'

'I've got surgery until midday, then a bite to eat, then I'm at the maternity hospital all afternoon.'

'So you won't be back late?'

'I've got evening surgery, remember?'

'Oh yes, of course. Phil . . .'

'What?'

'I know you probably can't – but do you think you could stay for a bit? Just for an hour or so? I do feel so awful.'

Annoyance crossed his face, quickly suppressed by concern. 'You know I can't. I've got a roomful of patients waiting for me, and Dr Ingoldby—'

'It's all right,' she said quickly, wishing she hadn't asked. Now all she wanted was for him to go. She couldn't stand him sitting there, telling her why he couldn't stay.

'You'll feel better once the aspirin starts working. Why not have a day in bed? I'll give you a ring mid-morning, to see how you are.'

'Don't do that. I might be asleep.'

He nodded and stood up. He wasn't happy. 'If you're really ill, Isabel . . .'

'No. It's only a headache. You go.'

She heard the front door of the house close and his car start up. She listened until the sound of the engine died away, and then she sat up. It was stifling under this eiderdown. She shoved the mass of it over to Philip's side of the bed, but she pushed too hard and the thing slid to the floor.

Philip hadn't had time to light the fire, although she'd heard him riddling the kitchen stove and shovelling in coke. The flat was cold. She clasped herself, shivering. She knew what she was going to do – she was pretending to herself, delaying the moment.

Isabel got out of bed and picked her way across the lino to the chair. She lifted the greatcoat and held it to her, inhaling its smell. She pressed the woollen cloth to her lips, and then climbed back into bed, spreading the greatcoat over herself. It's broad daylight, she told herself. He won't come now. She sighed and turned over, crossing her arms over her breasts and drawing up her knees. Now she felt safe. Now warmth was creeping through her, into the core of her body. She fell into a deep, dreamless sleep.

There was no knocking. She woke because there was a weight beside her, pressing into her body. Alec was sitting on the bed, where Philip had been.

'I hope you don't mind,' he said. 'The door was open, so I came in. I didn't mean to scare you.'

'I'm not scared,' she said.

'I had to come. There isn't much time,' he explained. 'Ops were scrubbed last night, after the briefing. Everyone was pretty browned off. It's one thing when you get a stand-down in the morning, but at six o'clock . . . We'll be on for sure tonight. We've done our air test—'

'Why was it scrubbed?'

'Bloody Met bods playing silly buggers again. We should have gone. All this hanging about is no good.' He rattled out the words angrily. He looked as if he hadn't slept. There were stains of shadow under his eyes, and the twitch over his right cheekbone was back.

'I wondered why you didn't come,' she said.

'I shouldn't be here now,' he said. 'I've got the bike outside, I'd better get weaving.'

'Wait, I'll come out with you.'

She pulled on her dressing gown, tied it tightly and smoothed back her hair. She was decent. 'I'll come to the front door,' she said.

'Better not come outside,' he agreed. 'Walls have eyes in this place.'

'You mean ears.'

'Do I?' He stared at her, completely distracted. He wasn't really here at all, she understood that. He was thinking about his kite and the ground crew who would be working on it now, bombing up and armouring, checking and rechecking. He should be there.

'Why did you come here?' she asked him, and in answer he brushed her cheek with his finger.

'Oh, I don't know,' he said, and then, his blue eyes darkening, fixing hers, 'I had to see you.'

She nodded. She wouldn't reach out for him. She remembered the games she and Philip used to play with magnets, pushing them away from one another. It was like that. There was a field around him that she couldn't cross.

'I just thought I'd like to see you,' he said again, 'but I've got to get back.'

'I know you have.' She opened the door to the hall

and peered upstairs. Nothing stirred. He was already at the front door, tugging the handle, but the door wouldn't budge.

'What's the matter? Is the lock jammed?'

The Yale moved easily, but the door remained locked. He looked upwards. 'No wonder, there's a ruddy great bolt on it.'

The door was locked and bolted, but Alec had come in. He hadn't knocked on the window or rung the bell. He tugged at the bolt, but it wouldn't give way. Suddenly he swore, and jerked his hand away. As he nursed his hand, she saw blood. One big drop splashed onto the tiled floor, and then another. The bolt hadn't moved.

'I'll try,' she said, stretching up.

'You'll hurt yourself,' he said, and pushed her aside. He went at the bolt again, roughly, jamming it further in, she thought. She itched to have a go at it herself but the state he was in, she didn't dare. More drops of blood fell and she got a handkerchief out of her dressing-gown pocket. 'Let me tie this round it for you. That bolt's rusty – you don't want to get rust in the cut—'

'For God's sake, Issy!'

He had almost shouted it. 'Alec!' she said, 'Don't!' but it was too late. Upstairs, there was the rattle of a bolt being drawn back, and then a door opened.

HELEN DUNMORE

Isabel didn't dare turn. If the landlady came down she would see Isabel in her dressing gown with a strange man. But Alec looked up, past Isabel, towards the landing. She heard the intake of his breath. His face froze.

Isabel, too, looked up. There was the landlady, in her grey pinafore, with her hair scragged back. She was stock-still, her face white in the shadow, staring at Alec. She looked him up and down as if he were a thing, a creature, loathsome. She didn't even glance at Isabel. Slowly, deliberately, she walked to the landing banisters and gripped them. Alec stepped forward, until he was standing beneath her. She leaned forward, her body tipping until it seemed that she would fall, and then she spoke, but only to Alec.

'You didn't come,' she said. 'You said you'd come, and you never came.'

Isabel saw Alec start forward, as if to go up to her, but the landlady put out her hand to ward him off. Alec stared up at her. 'You weren't there,' he said, and then he raised one hand, as if to shield his eyes from the sight of her. And no wonder, thought Isabel. She was shrivelled, her face skull-like, her skin colourless as if the blood scarcely moved there any more. There was a long silence. Isabel could not take her eyes from them. The young officer with his head tipped back, the old woman looking down, engulfing him with her gaze. Isabel watched them as if she were watching a film. This Alec was a stranger. She could not believe that he had ever touched her. She knew that he didn't belong to her: he had never belonged to her.

The landlady's anger had gone quiet. She breathed out a slow, exhausted sigh. Very slowly, she put out one hand and held it towards Alec, but gropingly, as if she didn't believe she would ever reach him, and then she was still, as Alec was still. Isabel barely breathed. Alec and the landlady no longer seemed to know that there was anyone in the house but them. Isabel clenched her fists. She would make them see her. She would make them know her. Humiliation burned in her, as if she were a child, helpless in the face of her parents' storms. But she was not a child.

'Alec,' she said quietly, and put out her hand, but she couldn't touch him. The landlady's gaze slipped to Isabel's face, and then away. Had she seen her, or not seen her? There was no telling. The landlady turned at last, holding the banister to support herself. Slowly, bowed over, she made her way back into her flat. She looked like an old, old woman, struck by a blow from which she would never recover.

Alec was gone, and Isabel was alone in the hall. She looked down, expecting to see nothing, but the dark splash of blood was there on the tiles. She knelt beside it. She still had her handkerchief. She laid it over the tiles and then lifted it. The stain was dark red, and sticky on her fingers when she touched it.

Chapter Ten

Isabel threw back the bedclothes, pulled the curtains wide and opened the window. Cold air coursed in over her body and she felt its chill with satisfaction. Upstairs it was silent. She went into the kitchen, took the wooden cover off the bath and ran the water way past the painted line five inches from the bottom of the tub. The hot water gave out but Isabel let it run on, cold. She got in then lay back, let her hair sink, and then her face. She was completely underwater. She opened her eyes and looked up through the distorted surface. The bath was too small and her knees were bent up, hunched against the taps. She lay there until her lungs burned, and then surfaced, streaming with water and rubbing it out of her eyes.

She took the loofah and scrubbed herself fiercely until her skin was red. For the first time in weeks, she was wide awake. She got out of the bath and dried herself vigorously. Of course she had never slept with another man. It was a crazy fantasy. She'd been on her own far too much and had lost her sense of what was real and what was not. The war had been over for years. The aircrew had all gone back to their lives – if they still had them. The airfield was deserted.

She wiped steam from the mirror and peered at herself. Her face was rosy and her eyes were bright. She would dry her hair, put on a sensible skirt and jumper and her warm coat, and go into town to do her shopping. Later she would call on Janet Ingoldby and talk to her about joining a sewing circle. She would write a letter to the grammar school, offering her services for extra French conversation lessons. Surely Philip couldn't mind that.

'You've been completely off your head,' she told her mirrored image severely. 'It's high time you got a grip.'

Her aunt had once said that to her. Isabel had taken to not eating, after news began to trickle in about the camps where her parents had died. Her aunt had folded her arms and stood over her while Isabel sat there with a plate of apple crumble on the table in front of her. Charlie had already escaped. Her aunt had said, 'This isn't going to bring them back, Isabel. It's time you got a grip.' Isabel had glanced up at Aunt Jean's lips, pressed tightly together now that she'd finished speaking. There was grey at her temples. She reminded Isabel of someone, and then she knew who it was. Of course: her aunt was Dad's sister. Isabel had never thought of that properly before. Her aunt unsealed her lips again. 'We have to carry on,' she said. 'It's what they would have wanted.' An extraordinary feeling of relief filled Isabel, as if some black poison were being leached away. It was all right not to think. It was good not to feel. She dug her spoon into the apple crumble.

That night Isabel could not sleep. Philip had gone out again, to a child with Still's disease. She turned over and over in bed, cold in spite of the eiderdown. She knew that Alec wouldn't come. Philip was so good, such a good doctor, she thought drearily. Janet Ingoldby had been pleased to see her. She had given her a pot of last summer's gooseberry jam. It was a beautiful deep transparent red, with the seeds shining dark through it. Janet had held it up to the light with satisfaction. The jam had set exactly as it ought.

'When you think of how much fruit went to waste, because we couldn't get the sugar,' she said. 'During the war, I mean. But of course, you're too young; you wouldn't remember.'

'I remember,' Isabel had said.

She was so cold now that her teeth were chattering. The eiderdown might as well not be there.

'Carrot jam!' went on Janet Ingoldby scornfully. 'The Ministry of Food appeared to have got carrots on the brain, when any woman could have told them there were pounds of blackberries rotting in the hedges for want of the sugar to make bramble jelly. Have you ever tasted wild damson preserve, my dear?'

I'm so cold, thought Isabel.

'Cook has always made our own rose-hip syrup. It's a bit of a fiddle to get the seeds out, but the children enjoyed helping. Give them a teaspoon of rose-hip syrup morning and evening. There's no necessity for runny noses all winter.'

Isabel turned over and huddled herself in the centre of the icy bed. She was so tired, but she would never be able to get to sleep. Janet Ingoldby's voice drummed in her head '. . . Home preserving . . . Chilprufe vests . . . Dr Ingoldby is very fond of smoked haddock . . .'

She had got to get warm. Surely it couldn't do any harm to get the greatcoat, just for a minute . . .

But it wasn't on the chair. Isabel's heart beat fast with panic. She hadn't touched it, she knew she hadn't. It had lain folded on the chair when she last looked. But when was that? She concentrated, trying to grip the sight of the greatcoat through the fog of her memory. It had been there, she was sure of it, when she'd tidied the flat before Philip came home.

There it was, hanging from the hook on the back of the door. The door had swung back, hiding it. It must have been Philip who put it there. She would just lay it on the bed for a little while, and then, when she was warm, she would hang it up again. As she thought this, Janet Ingoldby's voice stopped, as if someone had lifted the needle from the surface of a record.

Isabel dreamed. Alec's face emerged from the darkness in front of her, and hung there. It was appalling, so disfigured by anguish that she wanted to turn away but could not. His eyes were like caves. She touched his sleeve but he seemed not to feel her hand. She reached up to kiss him and bring him back to her. He turned away. She knew he was thinking of tonight. He was afraid. They'd been coned on the last trip to the big city. He did his stuff and by a miracle he got them away, but that doesn't happen twice. All those searchlights locked on to you so you could read a bloody book by them while you waited for the shell-burst to blow you out of the sky. Haul the kite into a screaming dive until it sounds as if every rivet is about to burst open. The lights tracking and you pinned against the darkness, spread out, the target for everything. They got out of it that time but it wouldn't happen again.

'I know,' she said over and over, trying to get to where he was, but he said, 'You don't,' and brushed her hand away.

She woke to the noise of Lancs. They were taking off at two-minute intervals. The wind must have changed because they were close to the town as they circled to gain altitude before they headed south-east. One and then another and then another and then another. The air filled and rumbled with their thunder. They were almost over the house, so low that if she could look up through the roof and then the fuselage she would see Alec with his flight engineer just behind him and to his right. And the huge pregnant Lanc with its bellyful of bombs passed over.

He'd gone. This was the twenty-seventh op. This one and three more to go until the end of the tour. It had begun. Alec had climbed out of the crack of time where he met Isabel over and over again, between the twenty-sixth and twenty-seventh op. The crew of poor old bloody Katie were off on their trip to the big city.

* * *

She had to go out to the airfield. Philip wouldn't be home yet, perhaps not until morning. Quickly she dressed and scribbled a note: 'Couldn't sleep, darling, gone out for a breath of fresh air.' She grabbed the torch that hung by the door in case of power cuts, and bent to lace her stout walking shoes. She was about to take her coat from the stand when she paused. After a moment's thought she took the greatcoat from the bed, put it on and fastened it. It was too big and came down almost to her ankles. There would be no one to see it, and it would keep her warm.

She spread margarine onto kitchen paper and greased the bolt on the front door of the house. It slid back easily. She stepped outside and closed the door behind her, very gently. There was almost no sound, but even so she waited, tense, listening. Nothing stirred and no lights came on upstairs. She crept down the steps. The street lamp had been turned off and no lights showed at any windows, but there was a moon, half full, with thin clouds racing over it.

'It's the blackout,' said Isabel to herself, and everything made perfect sense. There was enough moonlight to see her way: she wouldn't need her torch. She saw other, shadowy figures scurrying along, close to the walls, as if they were afraid. No one spoke to her or even glanced in her direction.

She turned the way she knew, which led to open country. Soon the houses and the bulk of the minster had fallen behind her. The country lane was wide, and freshly Tarmacked. She kept to its edge. A couple of times, lorries pounded past her, towards the airfield. She walked as fast as she could, keeping herself from breaking into a run. Her heart thudded with terrible urgency. She had to get there quickly but she didn't know why. Now the moon shone on the hedges and through the gates she saw wide fields. The landscape was bluish, thickly shadowed. A vixen screamed and Isabel jumped, even though she knew what it was. She wanted to be silent, a shadow, unnoticed. She paused to rest against a tree, and propped herself there, waiting. She knew it wasn't time yet. Hours must pass before the first bomber returned. She was folded into the night, waiting, wrapped inside the greatcoat.

She was at the perimeter fence. She knew that it was long after midnight. Now, in the winter darkness, the whole base was alive. A Lanc was taxiing in from the runway to dispersal. A crew bus jolted down the perimeter road in front of her, its engine mute against the thunder of the Lanc. For an instant she caught the profile of the WAAF who was driving. Ground crew swarmed as sound swelled in the distance again. There was more than one Lanc up there. They were in the circuit, waiting their turn to land. They were coming down the staircase of the sky, descending one by one towards the airfield. The thunder of them went through her, and she looked up, thinking she saw a vast shadow against the darkness of the sky. The control tower blinked. She saw the aircraft's landing lights as it came down the sky towards her, then it dipped towards the runway lights, bounced, settled and was down. The ground shook to its incoming roar.

Again and again the sky thickened with engines. One by one the Lancasters came in and taxied to dispersal. Crew buses passed her and she thought of the men hunched over their cigarettes, on the way to debriefing. She tried to think that Alec was among them, but the knot in her stomach wouldn't ease.

Now it was quieter. A straggler came in, and then another. She waited, tense with fear. He had to come now. There was only so much fuel and so many more minutes in the air. Unless he'd diverted – unless K-Katie was damaged – unless . . .

She couldn't see clearly. She blinked, but the fog wouldn't lift. It was rolling in from the east, great bales of it like wool, hiding the runway then swirling away again. Those bloody Met bods, she heard in her head. Got it wrong again.

They would tell him. He would abort the landing, go round, head for another airfield.

She heard it lumbering down the sky. It sounded all wrong. It was a Lanc but the engines weren't making the safe Merlin roar she would know anywhere, in her sleep even. They were jagging at the air, trying to cut through it, coughing, stuttering, and then suddenly they bellowed as if the pilot had forgotten to switch off the superchargers and the Lanc was coming down too fast, too steep, too close.

A brilliant light came on at the end of the runway. 'It's the chance light,' she said aloud. She knew what that was for. He had got to land and so they were giving him the light that was strong enough to burn through the fog. He hadn't enough fuel to reach another airfield, or else there was too much damage. The fog swirled clear and for a second she saw lights, figures and then the vast wallowing shadow of the Lanc as it swooped for the runway. But it would not go down. The engines screamed as the thing passed over her, fifty feet above her head. He had missed the runway. He was pushing the throttles forward as far as they would go, trying to get power, trying to lift her over the admin block and the hangars. The black thing clawed at the sky, went up, hung there roaring, then stuttered, stalled and plunged out of sight beyond the airfield.

There was absolute silence. She didn't think she heard the explosion. The air around her gathered itself, solidified, became a wall. It pulsed, breaking against her body again and again. She was falling forward. She was on the ground, with her face in wet grass.

Chapter Eleven

When she reached the house, there was no car outside. Philip must still be with the patient. She looked up and down the street. It was the same night, still going on endlessly. No one was about.

She let herself in quietly, and blinked in the sudden light. The landlady was sitting on the stairs. She looked up at Isabel, seeing her fully this time, her gaze sharp. She looked tired, but somehow satisfied. Like a cat, thought Isabel, that knows it has killed and will not be hungry for a while.

'It's done, then,' said the landlady.

'What do you mean?'

'You know what I mean.'

Isabel folded her arms. You won't get away with that, she thought. She was bold now, and she could ask what she wanted, because no one else would ever know.

'Was he killed?' she asked.

'Of course he was killed. They were all killed.'

'All the crew?'

The landlady's top lip lifted, showing her teeth. 'I'm not talking about them,' she said.

'Then who are you talking about?'

'I'm tired. I'm going to bed. Don't bother waiting up, he won't come back. And you can take off that coat. It doesn't belong to you.'

Isabel looked down at herself. Of course, she was still wearing the greatcoat. 'It belongs to me as much as it belongs to you,' she said. The landlady got up stiffly, banged her hands together, turned and went upstairs. She didn't look back.

It was quarter to seven. There was no point in going to bed now. And Philip still not home . . . Fear gnawed at her. He knew everything, and he had left her. He had found himself somewhere else to live. He would never come back to her. She sat at the table, too tired to make a cup of tea or light the fire. Slowly, a late winter dawn crept to the windows. In a minute she would take off the greatcoat and fall into sleep, and everything that had happened would disappear, like the substance of a dream. She knew that the landlady was right, and Alec would not come back. Why should he? He had done everything he had come to do. *I'm not talking about them,* the landlady had said. So there was something else, Isabel thought, and I must find it out.

When the telephone rang, her hand went to it smoothly. It was Philip, sleepy and apologetic. The child's condition had deteriorated, and he had been at the hospital. It had been so late that they had made up a camp-bed for him; he hadn't wanted to disturb Isabel. He might as well go straight to surgery, and he would be home at lunchtime, he promised. He had the afternoon off. They could go out for a drive, he thought, into the country. Would she like that?

'Yes,' she said, clutching the receiver close. 'I'd like that.'

She slept for a couple of hours, then dressed carefully, brushed her hair and coiled it into a chignon. She applied powder and dark-red lipstick. Now she looked older, and firm of purpose. She was a doctor's wife, in her tweed coat, busy and preoccupied. She pinned on her hat, picked up her shopping list and basket, and walked through the hall without glancing up at the landing.

Nothing could frighten her today. She went past the little groups of gossiping women in the market-place, without a tremor. She pointed out the bruised apple that the stall-keeper was about to slip into her bag. The butcher looked at her, and put down the fatty chops he had been about to weigh out for her. She didn't care what they thought of her any more, and they knew it.

'My dear!' It was Janet Ingoldby. She took Isabel's arm as if they were the oldest of friends. 'I heard that you weren't well.'

'I'm perfectly well.'

'They say that the cobbler's child is never shod.' Janet's smile was kind, but curious. 'We must make sure that Philip looks after you.'

'He looks after me very well,' said Isabel coolly.

'Of course.' The other woman hesitated. She feels it too, thought Isabel. She knows that she can't get at me any more.

'I'm going to give French conversation lessons at the grammar school,' Isabel said aloud. 'A few hours a week, to keep my hand in.'

'Philip said you had lived abroad.'

'I went to Bordeaux with a French family, when I was nineteen. They wanted their children to learn English.'

'How brave of your mother to let you go!'

'Not really,' said Isabel. 'She was dead.'

'Oh my dear, I'm so sorry, I had no idea, Philip never said . . .'

'It's not a secret. My parents were in Singapore

when it fell, and they were captured by the Japanese. She almost survived; she didn't die until 1945. It was terribly bad luck,' said Isabel, looking straight at Janet Ingoldby, daring her to say any of the things people said.

Janet Ingoldby took a step back, and her hand dropped from Isabel's arm. 'Oh dear,' she said, 'The war . . .' and she shook her head, looking down.

Isabel, too, looked down, her anger spent. What did she know of Janet or what she might have suffered? You were angry, she told herself, because of the way she kept saying 'Philip'. You wanted to pay her back.

'It was a long time ago,' Isabel said.

'I know. But some things never seem to stop happening, do they?' said Janet Ingoldby quietly. A shutter lifted, and for a second her grey eyes were clear and penetrating. 'You must look after yourself,' she said. The shutter fell again, and she said busily, 'Well, I must be going. Mrs Daniels needs more Cardinal Red for the kitchen floor. Why she never tells me when she knows it's about to run out, I can't think . . .'

Isabel knew where to go now. As she'd hoped, there were no other customers in the grocer's. The grocer's wife was sorting broken biscuits from whole, and she looked up with a flattering smile when she saw Isabel. Isabel took out her list and laid it on the counter.

'Will you have your order sent?'

'No, I'll wait. There's nothing heavy.'

The woman seemed glad of her custom today. Soon she was rattling away with her stories as she reached for a packet of tea, and then went over to the bacon machine. Isabel sat on the stool provided, and began to steer the conversation. They moved easily through food shortages, back to rationing and the war.

'I heard that one of the bombers coming back from Germany crashed at the airfield,' said Isabel. The grocer's wife turned to her, one hand still on the slicer, her face lit with an extraordinary blend of disbelief, relish for drama, and satisfaction at being the one to tell the story.

'She's not told you then.'

'Who?'

'Your landlady. Well, it's no wonder, I'd keep quiet about it if I were her. She calls herself Mrs Atkinson these days, but her married name was Bardsley. She used to live out at Stainthorpe, at the farm there. It's no more than a mile from the airfield, if it's that. Her husband and the babby were in the farmhouse that night, when one of the aircraft tried to land in the fog. It was coming back from a raid on Berlin, they said, and it had flak damage to the engines. It came right down on the farmhouse. Ploughed it into the ground. You can still see the scar.'

'Was it a Lancaster?'

'It was all Lancasters here, barring a few Halifaxes. Hallibags they called them. My friend was working nights in the officers' mess and she heard it come down. They all thought it was going to hit the buildings. She threw herself on the floor – she thought she was bound to die – but it went over. And then they were thinking he's cleared it, he's cleared it – and then everything went still. She said the explosion seemed to come ever so long after. Every soul in that farmhouse was killed – but *she* was in town. She had the same house then, you know, the one you're in at the minute. Her auntie left it to her, and she took lodgers. There was always people wanting somewhere to live. But she had two rooms on the ground floor for herself. The tale was, she was looking after the lodgers.' The grocer's wife was leaning right over the counter now and her eyes were bright. 'There was a lot went on in the war, with the men away for years on end, and you had to turn a blind eye, but even so – *her* man wasn't away. He was in a reserved occupation. She would stay over, you know, in town. She was fawce, she was. Her husband had no idea what was going on, apparently.'

'But what about the baby?'

'You may ask. She never went back to Stainthorpe, not even for the funeral. They were buried together, her husband and the child, although when I say "buried" – it's a question what there was to bury. And there was the girl who lived with them and helped with the little one. She was only sixteen,' said the grocer's wife, lingeringly.

'Was it a girl, or a boy – the baby?'

'A boy. A lovely little boy by all accounts. I never saw him. She never brought him into town. Her husband's brother got the land and he built hisself a new house, the far end of the land from where the old one stood. They don't have anything to do with her, the family. It was them as set the stone for the husband and the babby and she's never gone within a mile of the grave. It's a queer house you're lodging in.'

Isabel found she was holding on to the counter edge, to steady herself. The stool wobbled.

'You do look poorly,' said the grocer's wife. 'Shall I get you a glass of water?'

'No,' said Isabel. She drew in her breath slowly, filling her lungs. There was sweat under her arms and in the small of her back. She must recover herself. She must not betray herself. 'I'd like the bacon medium-cut,' she said coolly, 'and please put in half a pound of digestives.'

'Plain or chocolate?' said the grocer's wife, offended.
'Plain, please.'

They were all killed. That was what the landlady had
said. All the crew killed, and the baby, the landlady's
husband and the girl who looked after the baby. That
was what Isabel had heard and seen, as she waited by
the perimeter fence.

She walked home slowly, carrying her basket. She
ought to have let the grocer's boy bring it later.
She felt very ill. The grocer's wife had been offended,
but she'd been curious too. She'd looked Isabel up
and down. That was the trouble when you came to a
new place as a stranger. You didn't know anything
about the past. You didn't know what had made
people as they were.

The noise of her own blood in her ears was like the
landlady's footsteps, going faster and faster.

'Isabel!' said Philip, jumping from his chair and
putting his arm around her.

'I'm all right.'

'You don't look all right. Sit down.'

'I walked too fast, that's all – and the shopping's
heavy.'

'How many times have I told you not to go lugging that basket back? They've got a boy to deliver.'

'I know. I was only going for a few things.'

She leaned back and closed her eyes.

'Why do you rush at things? Why can't you look after yourself?' he exclaimed angrily. Isabel said nothing. She was silenced by this view of herself. Was this what he'd always thought? At last he said, more quietly, 'I've been worried about you. I was thinking – should I ask Dr Ingoldby to examine you?'

'Dr Ingoldby!'

'He's very good.'

'I'm sure he is.'

'I was wondering . . . if there was any possibility . . .'

Her eyelids snapped open. He looked shy, not like a doctor at all. Her Philip. Oh God, she thought, he thinks I might be pregnant.

I might be pregnant. She thought of the hut, and Alec. With a huge effort, she collected herself and smiled up at her husband. 'It's far too soon to be sure,' she said, hating herself as his face lit up. He knelt by the chair and she felt the beating of his heart as he pulled her against him, clumsy with love and hope. He stroked back her hair. She thought: This is what he has been working for. This is everything that he wants. I can't—

The Lancaster crashed. They were all killed. He

won't ever come back. It was the landlady who did it, it was all her doing. She made me find that greatcoat. She made it all happen. If she couldn't have him herself then she was going to have him through me. No wonder she was walking overhead. She knew what she wanted. She hated him for what happened but she never stopped wanting him. She was going to get him back any way she could.

It was always between the twenty-sixth and twenty-seventh ops, every time I saw him. He'd got through so much, why shouldn't he start believing he was going to get through it all?

He's dead and gone, she told herself. The war has been over for years. I'm going to have Philip's child.

'We can't stay here,' Philip was saying. 'I'll go and see the bank manager tomorrow.'

'It may be nothing,' Isabel warned, but it made no impression.

'Whatever happens, it's time we had a home of our own,' he said.

She loved the look on his face, but she feared it too. All that purpose and protection was folding around her, but it could turn against her too. She had only to open her mouth and he would hate her. She was afraid that some force stronger than herself, some demon of self-destruction, would put words into her mouth and make her speak out. Philip wasn't the kind of man who would be able to forgive her. Where he trusted, he did so implicitly; he could not forgive betrayal. But I've done nothing, she told herself. It's not real, none of it is real. It's the landlady. The war has been over for years, but she's still obsessed with it. She won't let go.

Isabel took Philip's hand, turned it over and folded her own into it. 'Sometimes I'm afraid we'll be here for ever,' she said, 'with Mrs Atkinson walking to and fro all night, until we're old and grey.'

'That won't happen. I'll make enquiries. The bank manager's wife is a patient of Dr Ingoldby's. If people like us can't get a mortgage . . .'

Isabel sat at the dressing table, creaming her face before bed. She could hear Philip whistling as he riddled the kitchen stove. In the mirror she saw the greatcoat, lying on her side of the bed. Had she put it there? She didn't think so. She got up, folded the greatcoat and took it into the living room. She would put it back in the cupboard, where it belonged. No. That wasn't enough. It must be got out of the flat entirely, but for tonight the cupboard would have to do. Isabel fetched a chair, clambered up, opened the cupboard wide and shoved the coat as far back as it would go.

169

'What on earth are you doing?' asked Philip. She turned and there he was in the doorway, watching her.

'Putting the coat away. I don't need it now that we've got the eiderdown.'

'You shouldn't climb like that.' He held out his hands to her. She took them, and he jumped her down lightly, taking her weight.

In the night, she woke. The weight was on her again, pushing her down. She put out her hand and felt the thick woollen cloth. Terror crawled over her skin, and she lay dead still, not daring to reach out or speak to Philip. Stiff, staring into the dark, she lay until sleep swallowed her again. In the morning Philip said, 'I thought we were getting rid of that thing. Don't tell me you got up in the middle of the night and dug it out of that cupboard again.'

'I'm going to wrap it up and put it in the dustbin.'

'You can't do that, Isabel. It's not ours.'

'I don't care. If she wants it that much, she ought to come and take it.'

'Who?'

'The landlady, of course. It's hers.'

'I daresay the old girl's forgotten all about it.'

'Take it to the surgery, Phil. I don't want it in the flat.'

'Wouldn't it be simpler just to take it upstairs to her?'

Tears sprang to her eyes.

'All right, all right,' he said, 'I'll do it. Don't get in such a state.'

'Put it in the boot now.'

'For heaven's sake, Is, I'm still in my dressing gown, in case you hadn't noticed.'

'I'll do it, then.'

Philip never locked the boot. She flew down the steps, holding the greatcoat out as if it were burning, turned the handle and thrust the thing inside.

She walked slowly up the steps. The cold went through her, sharp, piercing, alive. It was over. The coat was gone and soon they would leave the flat behind, and the landlady, and never see her again. She knew that she could sleep now. There would be no tap on the window, or drone of heavy bombers circling for altitude. It was over.

She heard the landlady's words again: *Don't bother waiting up, he won't come back.*

No, he won't come back, Isabel thought. For a moment she felt him again, against her, entering her as the sound of the planes entered her ears. She smelled oil and sweat and the faint tang of his oxygen mask on his breath. His fingers tasted of nicotine and they trembled and then steadied as they touched her, tentatively at first and then stroking her skin with infinite gentleness, as if he hadn't believed he would ever touch a woman's face again.

Chapter Twelve

For weeks the sun had shone. Everyone expected the weather to break, but each morning the sun burned off the early mist and by eight o'clock it was warm enough for Isabel to take her first cup of tea outside. The berries on the rowan were turning red. Everything was ripening early this year.

Michael woke at five, with the birds. The days were long, and Isabel lived them mostly outdoors. They hadn't tamed the garden yet. The borders had been ghosts of themselves, sunk in weeds, the lawn a field, and the orchard, where one day they planned to keep hens, was still a mass of briar and bramble. The old woman who had owned the house lived there alone for years, retreating until she occupied only a single downstairs room. She had no bathroom, and only a single cold-water tap in the kitchen. The range hadn't been used for a decade; old Mrs Gawthorpe had lived to ninety-four on bread, cheese and raw onions. There were no relations apart from a nephew in Canada, who was almost seventy himself and only wanted the place sold. It was Dr Ingoldby who told Philip about the house before it was auctioned.

They borrowed from Isabel's aunt, and from the bank. The house was everything that Philip had ever wanted. The work it needed could all be done in time.

'I want the children to grow up here,' he said.

He said 'the children', as if there were already a houseful of them. Isabel was pregnant with Michael then. She was booked into the maternity hospital for the birth, but she never got there. The baby took them by surprise, for he was two or three weeks early, according to Philip's calculations. He was a big, fair infant, weighing eight and a half pounds, and his eyes were blue. All newborns had eyes of that colour, Philip said. Later, they would darken.

'He's very fair,' said Isabel's aunt when she came to visit.

'Yes,' said Isabel.

'Of course, Richard was blond when he was a little boy.' She said 'Richard', not 'your father', as if she and Isabel were equals now. 'I used to be so jealous. People thought blond curls were absolutely marvellous, in those days. But Richard's didn't last.'

'I expect Michael will go darker too.'

She felt so sure of herself when she was holding the baby that she didn't care what anyone said. He was an easy baby, everybody said so. Janet Ingoldby declared that Michael was a fluke, and Isabel would get a shock when the next one came along. Michael fed hungrily and seldom cried. He had a way of looking at Isabel when she was buttoning her blouse after a feed, as if they were in perfect agreement: *We're in this together. You look after me, and everything will be all right.*

'He likes it here,' Isabel said, stroking Michael's cheek, still not quite believing that this peaceful child could be her own.

'Of course he does,' said Philip.

'He likes the garden. When I put his pram under the rowan tree, even if he's not asleep, he'll watch the leaves for hours.'

Each weekend, Philip mowed the rough, bumpy lawn and dug the vegetable garden. While Michael slept, Isabel cleared borders and planted lavender and rosemary; strong things that would thrive. She scattered marigold seed and love-in-a-mist. Every so often she would pause to listen out for the baby, but he rarely cried.

A woman came up from the village to scrub the place once a week. Janet Ingoldby was horrified that Isabel didn't have more help.

'It's fine. I can manage,' said Isabel.

'My dear, you're so brave. But it's been hopeless since the war. They all go off and get jobs in town.'

Michael filled Isabel's mind, and soothed it. She lived outdoors in cotton dresses, her arms and legs brown. She brought his playpen out onto the grass and gave him his toys one by one while he lay kicking in the shade. Later, he would sit up with a perfectly straight back, examining a rag book or a giraffe that squeaked. He was nine months old now, and could pull himself up to stand at the railings of his playpen. Day after day the sun shone, the grass tanned, the leaves turned a darker, duskier green.

The village was two miles away, but Isabel never wished it closer. Out here, there was no one to watch her. She was doing what was expected of her, and so she was left alone: she was the doctor's wife, with her baby and her garden. The delivery van from the village shop found Isabel up a ladder with a paintbrush in her hand, as often as not. Or she would be digging, with her hair tied up in a kerchief, and the baby on his blanket nearby. The vicar called, and Isabel didn't say that Philip was an atheist; instead, she made tea and talked about the long hours Philip worked. The vicar sat back in his chair in the cool, dark kitchen and rested his eyes on Isabel as she moved about, filling the kettle, bringing cream from the larder for his scones.

'Your husband is a lucky man,' he said. She looked at him, startled, and he added quickly, 'These scones are light as a feather. Take it from me, I'm a connoisseur.'

'You must be,' she replied, and her hair swung forward over her face, hiding it.

He kept seeing that swing of hair, loose and shining and also cool somehow, as he drove back to the village in the glare of the afternoon. A nice young family, he would say to his wife.

The more Isabel listened, the more she heard. A tractor far away, and the scream of gulls that came inland to feed from the furrows. The high, invisible skirling of larks in the summer sky when she lay on her back in the meadow that belonged to the house, although it was leased to a farmer who mowed it for hay. The drip of the kitchen tap, the buzz of a bumblebee in the depths of a foxglove flower, and Michael's crooning as he settled himself to sleep. There were a thousand sounds.

'You're sure it's not too quiet for you out here? You aren't lonely?' Philip asked in the first months, but she always said no, and smiled to reassure him, so that he stopped asking. The thought of her tutoring French at the grammar school had fallen away, like everything else from the early months of their marriage. She had Michael, and there would be more children, she was sure of it. The house and garden would fill with them. The back door would always be open, so that she could keep an eye on them, and listen for their quarrels and laughter.

She had told her aunt that she wanted a large family.

'It's what people seem to be doing these days,' said Aunt Jean.

'What do you mean?'

'Well – the war,' her aunt had explained briskly, as if it shouldn't need to be spelled out. 'I only had Charlie. Your parents only had you. It wasn't uncommon at the time, but now . . . It's to do with replacement, I suppose.'

'Replacement . . .'

'It's a natural instinct,' said her aunt.

'I never thought of it like that.'

'I don't suppose you did.'

The word stayed in Isabel's head for weeks. *Replacement.* But the frightening thing was how easily the world got on without the dead. All those thousands – *millions* – yet somehow the houses were full of people, just the same. The dead were gone. They were thought of, but the year rolled round, and then there was another year, and you couldn't live in the past.

But the dead, of course, couldn't feel that; if they

felt anything. They had missed so much, years and years of life . . . How could they not feel resentment? The years that were rolling on were the very years that they were missing. They must want them back . . .

No, she wouldn't think of that. Instead, Isabel snuffed the warm smell of Michael's skin. It was so soft; you couldn't think of anything that was like it. People said silk, or rose petals, but that was nonsense. Michael was here, in her arms, while all those others were not. Even her own mother, if she saw Isabel, might become hungry: *She has everything, and I have nothing.*

No mother would think that about her own child, Isabel told herself quickly. Her mother would be happy to see Isabel with Michael. She would never begrudge them their life, because she was alive in them.

How black the shadow was, under the pear tree that hadn't been pruned for years – decades – and yet it still kept valiantly throwing out blossom, and bending down its branches with long drops of immature fruit.

It was early August, and Philip was out in the garden with Michael. Isabel wasn't well. It was nothing definite, but she was pale and tired, she was sleeping badly and had lost her appetite. Perhaps she was pregnant again? But it was too early to be sure.

'You go to bed,' he said, when she couldn't eat anything at lunch. 'A couple of hours' peace is what you need. I'll keep an eye on Michael. I'll have to leave at three for afternoon surgery, but I should be home by seven. We can have a scratch supper.'

A scratch supper! Another of Dr Ingoldby's expressions, no doubt, thought Isabel wearily, as she climbed the stairs. She lay down on top of the covers. It was too hot even for a sheet. People were starting to say that the weather was unnatural. There was talk of prayers for rain. She smiled to herself at the thought of the vicar as a rain-maker.

The bed felt as if it were floating away beneath her. She watched the sun patches quiver on the white walls. How her head ached. Perhaps she *was* pregnant. Next year there might be another baby. She could only imagine another Michael, as fair and peaceful as the first, waiting patiently for her to open the gate of life and let him in. Well, she could manage that. She had found pregnancy easy, and birth too, against all her expectations. It was only this feeling that kept gaining on her, as if she were living underwater, and the world were swaying around her . . .

Isabel dozed, and dreamed shallowly, skipping the surface of sleep. Sometimes she heard Michael, sometimes Philip's deeper tones. He was always careful with Michael. She could trust him. He wasn't one of these fathers who thought a baby needed to be toughened up by hurling it into the air or clapping his hands in its face.

I'll go down, thought Isabel, seized with sudden tenderness for Philip. He gets so worried when I'm ill.

The dazzle of the afternoon sun hit her as she stepped out of the door. She shaded her eyes and squinted into the baking heat of the garden. There was Philip, patiently digging dandelions out of the yellowing grass. But the playpen was empty. Her gaze swivelled. No, it was all right, there Michael was, sitting on the—

Her breath caught. She felt the pounding of her heart.

'Philip!'

'What's the matter?' He was across to her in seconds, his arm round her. 'You shouldn't have come down. It's too hot for you out here.'

'Philip – the greatcoat.' Her voice was a whisper. 'You've put him on the greatcoat.' She broke free of Philip's grip and ran across the grass. There was the baby, looking up at her out of those eyes that were such a deep blue that they were almost navy. He smiled, and waved his hands at her. She bent down, snatched him up and held him to her so tightly that even placid Michael wriggled in protest. She kicked the coat away as if it were on fire.

'Why did you bring that thing here? I told you to get rid of it.'

'For heaven's sake, Isabel, calm down. You're frightening Michael. I did take it to the surgery, but Mrs Ramsden came across it when she was cleaning out the hall cupboard. I thought I could use it for gardening, in the winter.'

'I don't want it in the house. I want you to burn it.'

'Don't be silly. I'll keep it out in the shed if you're so bothered about it.'

He was smiling at her, showing his teeth. *You fool,* she thought, *you fool,* and for a moment she hated him with every fibre of her being. But she mustn't show it. She would let him put the coat in the shed, and then she would get rid of it as soon as he'd gone. She could take a spade and bury it well away from the house, in a ditch, where the earth was soft. Michael would think that was an adventure.

'I've got quarter of an hour before surgery,' said Philip. 'Let's have some tea.'

There they were, the three of them, mother, father and child. Philip carried out the tea, and a sponge cake, and put their deckchairs in the shade of the medlar tree. Michael sat with his own piece of cake, smearing jam over his face, utterly content. The harshness of noon was past now; the light was becoming golden.

'You look better,' said Philip. He drank a second cup of tea, took another slice of cake, glanced at his watch.

'Don't go,' said Isabel.

He got up and kissed the top of her head. 'You know I've got to go. Will you be all right? Shall I ask Mrs Poole to come up for a couple of hours?'

'I'll be fine.'

'Oh, I forgot to tell you. You remember our old landlady?'

How could he possibly imagine she'd forgotten? 'Yes.'

'Cerebral haemorrhage.'

'What?'

'Bleeding in the brain tissue.'

'I know what it means. But what's happened – is she dead?'

'She's in hospital in York.'

'Oh . . . Will she . . . ?'

He frowned. 'She's not my patient, Is. But it's not usually a very bright outlook.'

Now she longed for him to go. She was so tired.

She could not think about the landlady, not now. She would take Michael upstairs with her and lie down for a while. Michael might drop off — he hadn't had his afternoon nap yet. Philip was wiping Michael's face and hands with the corner of his bib. The baby looked up at him and laughed.

'See you later, young man, look after your mother,' said Philip, tapping Michael on the nose, and he was gone, striding away across the rough grass. He turned the corner of the house and disappeared. She heard the car door clunk shut, and then the engine started.

Isabel picked up Michael and rocked him gently, to comfort herself, but he didn't want to be held. She wouldn't bother to go upstairs. She would just lie down on the blanket beside Michael and rest her eyes until it was time to make his bottle. It was cool here, in the shade . . .

The tree rustled, and something fell on her face. A leaf or an unripe fruit. Isabel rolled over, pushed her hair off her face and opened her eyes. Michael was sitting up beside her, crowing and stretching out his arms to the distance. She looked where he was looking, out of the shade and into the dazzle.

Alec was walking towards her, in his greatcoat

despite the heat of the day. As he crossed the lawn he smiled at Isabel, a warm, brilliant smile.

'I've been looking for you everywhere,' he said. He bent down and she smelled his smell: cigarette smoke, a trace of engine oil, the bitter tang of his oxygen mask. He lifted the baby from the blanket and cradled him in his arms. He handled Michael confidently, as if he had held him many times, and Michael, she could see, was happy with him. Isabel did not stir. She could not. The world was dissolving, breaking up around her. Dappled light glinted on the fairness of Alec's hair, and the air moved like water.

'I haven't got much time,' said Alec. 'I shouldn't be here. We're off again tonight.'

'You mustn't tell me that,' said Isabel.

'Don't you remember, you told me that you were a grave of secrets? I had to see you. Thank God for the old bike. I've only got a few minutes.' He took off his greatcoat, spread it on the grass next to the blanket and knelt on it. He was about to lower the child onto the coat, but Isabel grabbed his arm.

'Don't put him down on that!'

'Why on earth not?'

'It might be . . . it might be dirty.'

Alec shrugged but got to his feet again, still holding the baby. Isabel held out her arms to take him, but Alec began to fool with him, bouncing him, chucking him a little way into the air and catching him again, while Michael squealed with delight.

'Dance to your Daddy
My bonnie laddie
Dance to your Daddy
My little man'

sang Alec, and his eyes were on Isabel.

'Give him to me,' said Isabel sharply. 'My husband will be back soon.'

'That's where you're mistaken. He's out on the far field. I saw him on the tractor,' said Alec.

'What do you mean?'

'The farmer's in his den
The farmer's in his den
Eee Aye Eee Aye
The farmer's in his den . . .'

sang Alec.

'For God's sake,' said Isabel.

'I can sing something else if you prefer.'

'One of your mess songs, I suppose.'

'Don't worry, it's perfectly decent.

'We don't want to go to Chopland
We don't want to go at all

*We don't want to go to Chopland
Where our chances are f*** all . . .'*

'Sorry, darling. Not quite so decent after all. But it's Laney's song, not mine – you'll have to blame him.'

'You've got to go. He – my husband – he really will be back in a minute.'

'He won't be back until the light's gone. You've told me before that he won't waste a drop of daylight. He can plod up and down in his tractor for as long as he likes. What it is to be a man in a reserved occupation,' said Alec, and the tang of bitterness in his voice made Michael's face crumple.

'Alec, don't.'

'Listen, Lizzie. Briefing's at four. The gen is that it'll be the big city tonight for sure – that's more than seven hours, there and back again.'

'It might not be,' said Isabel quickly. 'You've had duff gen before.'

'You only have to look at the fuel load. Tell him you've got to go into town tonight. You can think of some excuse. I'll come to the flat, whatever happens. I'll be there as soon as I can after the debrief.'

Isabel's hair crisped at the roots with terror. She must not let him see. She must not antagonise Alec in any way, not while he held Michael in his arms.

He was back there, between the twenty-sixth and twenty-seventh ops. He hadn't got away after all.

Lizzie. Had it always been Lizzie he was looking for? When he first mouthed her name on the other side of the glass, she'd thought his lips were moving in the shape of her name: *Isabel.* But it might have been *Elizabeth* . . .

The landlady's presence thickened around her. It wanted to come in. It wanted to flood her once again with memories that weren't hers. It wanted to possess Alec through her.

The greatcoat, thought Isabel. It had opened the door for Alec again, and now he was here. The landlady had never let him lie. She had brought him back again and again. She walked and walked over that floor, until she had walked him back to her. If he couldn't be with her, then she would still have him through Isabel. She might be lying flat on her back in a hospital bed in York, but in her mind she was walking still.

The child. The landlady would have her child too. She would have her child again, through Isabel. *A lovely little boy by all accounts. I never saw him.*

There was Alec, with Michael in his arms, bending down his fair head to the child's fairness. Michael was so peaceful, gazing at the man whose eyes were the colour of his own. Gooseflesh rose on Isabel's arms, but she said, 'Give the baby to me a minute. I think he's wet.'

She said it so matter-of-factly that he simply handed Michael to her. She took him and felt his nappy. 'I thought so. I'll have to change him, Alec. Wait here.'

'But I can't stay long!' Alec burst out, and his face twisted. She saw the exhaustion etched into it again, the dark stains under his eyes, the twitch in his right cheek. He'd had enough and he knew it, but he was still trapped between the twenty-six and twenty-seventh ops. Death couldn't wipe the fear from his eyes. *Not while she still kept him coming back to her . . .*

'You shouldn't be here, Alec,' she said.

'I know that,' he said.

His arms were around her. He held her carefully, so as not to scare the child. He whispered in her ear: *Lizzie, Lizzie. Issy, Issy.* She thought: He would never have come to me like this, not in life. He would never have left the airfield, or his crew. *She* has almost got what she wanted. They are almost back together. The landlady, Alec, the child.

She felt herself drifting. It was true, the world was turning to water around her. Everything that she'd thought solid was drifting away. She could smell his smell. He had missed so much. He'd been outside for so long, in the dark and cold. Why not let him come in? Why not let it happen? Why not empty herself, and let the landlady return, so that Alec could stay? It was what Elizabeth Atkinson had wanted, year after year. She had walked that floor all night long, waiting and wanting, until she brought him back.

But what did she bring him back to? The worst days. Four more ops to go, and then tour expired, but he never allowed himself to think of that.

'You've got to press on.' He'd said that to Isabel, in those clipped words out of his weary face. He was so afraid. Isabel could see it now, in the way he held Michael, as if the baby were life itself, unbearably precious. *She* must have known how afraid he was. Afraid of what was coming, afraid of fear itself, afraid that he might not make it, might break down in front of his crew as they put their valuables into their lockers, and gave in the keys so that their lockers wouldn't have to be broken open if they failed to return.

Alec knew what the defences were like on the bombing run over Berlin. He'd been coned and got them out of it but you don't get that luck twice. That was what the landlady was making him return to, over and over: and now it was the worst day of all, with the night ahead of him. That wasn't love, thought Isabel. It was more like vengeance.

The world was turning to water. She could let go

now. Let herself sink, fall, go down endlessly until her mind was empty for someone else to occupy—

Michael cried. A small protest, the most he ever allowed himself. He didn't like the way she was holding him, or the way Alec was pressing so close. He wanted his bottle. Gently, Isabel disengaged herself. She stepped backwards, holding the child.

'You don't have to go into town after the debriefing,' she said. 'You can come here. It'll be all right: I'll make sure of it. He's going over to his brother's to help with the milking tomorrow. I'll tell him to sleep there, so he can make an early start. There will only be me and the baby here. I'll send the girl home. She'll be glad of a night off.'

'Are you sure?'

'Yes, I'm quite sure. You can come here, and I'll be waiting for you. It will be all right. It's much simpler than your going into town.'

He smiled at her. She saw the naked sweetness of it, the smile of a boy who hadn't gone through any of this yet, or maybe of a man who was beginning to believe that one day it might all be over for him. 'I do love you, you know,' he said.

'I know you do.'

'If it hadn't been for all this—'

'I know. It's all right.'

'Look at that, he's dropped off.'

It was true. Michael had fallen asleep between them.

'Must have a clear conscience,' said Alec.

'I should hope so.'

They both looked down at the sleeping baby. She wondered if Alec could see, as she did, the separateness of him. He wasn't Lizzie's, or Issy's. He was Michael. She would fight to the death for that.

'Let me take him,' said Alec, as if a sudden, unbearable impulse had rushed over him.

'No,' she said.

They were silent. It was all there between them, almost on the surface now: the life she held; the life he couldn't have again. All those others, millions of them, and the world had filled up and gone on without them.

'Better go,' said Alec, glancing again at his watch. 'I shouldn't be here at all.'

'Kiss me first.'

They kissed quickly, a light dry kiss of the kind lovers can afford when they know they will be together again within hours. He turned and walked out of the sunlight, into the shadow of the path that led to the overgrown orchard, and beyond it, to the lane. She didn't even try to see what he saw. She just watched him as he went, the fairness of him, the sun glinting on his head. He didn't turn back. She listened. After a while, sure enough, she heard his motorbike.

'I'll be out again tonight, I'm afraid,' said Philip over supper.

'Where?'

'The Eden baby's on its way. It's her third, but she's over forty and I'm not happy about her blood pressure.'

'All right.'

'You look a lot better than you did earlier.'

'I'm fine. How is the . . . I mean, Mrs Atkinson?'

'No change.'

The night wore on, warm, moonlit, full of drifting scent from the stocks Isabel had planted under the windows. It was too fine a night to be indoors. She lifted Michael from his cot and wrapped him in a shawl. He smelled of sleep and baby sweat. She pressed him close and went down the stairs without turning on the lights.

The garden was still. She walked over the dewy grass to the medlar tree and stood in its shelter, watching the house. The chirring of a hidden nightjar spilled from the orchard behind her. She listened, almost wishing that the baby would wake so that he could hear it too. The warm air stirred, smelling of grass.

Suddenly the sound of the nightjar was cut, as if the night had been sliced through. From the far distance there came the low rumble of engines, like an incoming storm. She knew them: they were Merlin engines. They were coming closer, beating their way in from the south-east. They didn't sound right. Quickly, she ran over the dewy grass, away from the house, through the tangled orchard. She huddled over Michael, listening intently and watching the house.

In the moonlight a woman appeared at her bedroom window. She had pushed aside the blackout blind and she was standing there, looking up at the sky. She was holding a white bundle. She, like Isabel, had her baby in her arms. The thunder of engines was coming closer now, searching them out.

Freezing air washed over Isabel. Before her eyes the clear summer moonlight thickened into fog. It was winter now, and the early hours of morning. Two o'clock, three o'clock perhaps. They had been all the way to the big city and now they were limping home. That sound must mean that the Lanc had engine damage. The noise swelled towards Isabel, rasping the sky, making the ground tremble. The Lanc was behind her, descending towards the airfield, coming in to land on the runway where the flare path was lit and the chance light waiting. But he could not get her down. Get down, you bitch, he said as the Lanc fought him and the runway slid past to the left of her groping wheels, and then the throttles were rammed forward with both of them holding it, him and Laney, K-Katie shaking as if she would shake herself to pieces and the two remaining engines screaming as she fought to climb and they cleared the admin block and they were over the trees and then the ground went up and the undercart, the fucking undercart—

The grey farmhouse with the green back door exploded as the Lanc came down.

Of such disasters, people usually said, 'At least they wouldn't have known anything.' There was a fraction of a second, maybe, when the inferno bloomed around Alec, before he felt it and was obliterated by it. But who knows? This time, there was nothing left of any of them. The fire slumped into ash, into earth, into grass, into speedwell and scarlet pimpernel. It was over.

* * *

A long time later, Isabel opened her eyes. The baby's shawl had slipped down over her arm, but it didn't matter. It was a summer's night, and when she touched Michael's bare feet, they were warm. She waded forward through the wet tangle of the orchard, until she was out on the lawn. Once again, the moon shone clear. The nightjar chirred. Now she was in the moon-shadow, under the medlar tree, with Michael in her arms. The air was still, but down on the grass the greatcoat's heavy cloth rippled, as if a night wind were walking under it.